THE TIME IT HAPPENED

Third Flatiron Anthologies
Volume 4, Spring 2015

Edited by Juliana Rew
Cover Art by Keely Rew

The Time It Happened
Third Flatiron Anthologies
Volume 4, Spring 2015

Published by Third Flatiron Publishing
Juliana Rew, Editor

Copyright 2015 Third Flatiron Publishing
ISBN #978-0692398203

Discover other titles by Third Flatiron:

(1) Over the Brink: Tales of Environmental Disaster

(2) A High Shrill Thump: War Stories

(3) Origins: Colliding Causalities

(4) Universe Horribilis

(5) Playing with Fire

(6) Lost Worlds, Retraced

(7) Redshifted: Martian Stories

(8) Astronomical Odds

(9) Master Minds

(10) Abbreviated Epics

License Notes

www.thirdflatiron.com

Contents

*****~~~~~*****

Editor's Note

by Juliana Rew

Our previous anthology skewed heavily toward fantasy and epic themes. In contrast, this edition, which calls upon the theme, "The Time It Happened," is almost entirely hard science fiction. We asked for tales that evoke an event that everyone remembers, or certainly would remember if it were to actually happen.

In reading submissions we were pleased to receive a number of time-tinkering stories, including a return of favorite character Dr. Leon Prinz in Martin Clark's intriguing alternate history recounting of the Apollo 11 mission in "False Footfall."

As every writer knows, it's well nigh impossible to get a tin foil hat story published, but you'll be glad to know we're publishing not one, but two! Ellen Denton's "Stilled Life" nicely complements Clark's offering.

Humans may have some exciting future events to look forward to as they reach for the stars, as in Richard Mark Ankers' "Armada of Snow," Evan Henry's "With Gilded Wings," and Jason Lairamore's "Kin Carriers."

We couldn't leave out Sputnik, of course. Thomas Canfield spins an engaging tale about who really won the space race in "Puppy Love."

There's a healthy helping of sobering "what-if" scenarios, including "Net War I" by Elliotte Rusty Harold, "Going Viral" by Dan Koboldt, and "Good to the Last Drop" by Wendy Nikel.

With the passage of time comes memories, which can be either heartbreaking, as in Atar Hadari's "Lincoln's Watch," or heartening, as in Larry C. Kay's "What Was Lost."

Anchoring the collection is "A Rock in the Air," an affecting tale about a man who is thrown forward in time by the explosion in Hiroshima and his ultimate decision to return home to be with his people.

Our flash humor offerings, "Blargnorff Industries New Employee Handbook Human Edition" by Dana Schellings, "The Zzzombie Apocalypse" by Mark Hill, and "Xenofabulous" by Amanda C. Davis," show the importance of proper behavior and attire as well as a good work ethic.

"The Time It Happened" proudly showcases an international group of new and established speculative fiction authors, who help us recall events as they could only happen in the mind's eye.

*****~~~~~*****

False Footfall

by Martin Clark

He lies like an eye-witness – Russian proverb

"But it didn't *happen* that way." I stared at the Google entry on my GP's laptop, conscious of the whine in my voice.

Doctor Mathers had the rueful smile/sympathetic tone combination down pat.

"Well, I'm afraid the rest of the world would have to disagree with you there, John. The Apollo Eleven disaster is one of those iconic moments in popular culture. Everyone knows where they were when the lander crashed, plus something like one-hundred-and-twenty million people watched it live on television."

I shook my head, unable to accept the evidence before my eyes. "No, it was a success, a complete success. They all got back safely."

"Apollo *Twelve* was the first successful landing, if a somewhat muted affair, and Apollo Thirteen recovered the bodies of Armstrong and Aldrin. I'm sorry, John, but that's just the way things are."

The pain behind my eyes kicked up a notch. I rubbed my temple. "I don't understand. What's wrong with me?"

My GP sat back. "Well, I could schedule an MRI, or refer you to a psychologist, but I'm certain what you're suffering from is Temporal Psychosis. . . " I must have blanched or something, as he quickly raised a hand, ". . . which, despite the serious-sounding name, is actually quite a mild condition. I see one or two cases a month, and they've all responded to a straightforward treatment regimen."

"But you're saying that I'm mentally ill?"

"Good God, man, no. You're simply part of that small group who suffer the side-effects of prolonged exposure to chronometric radiation. Once we identify the source, I'll be able to recommend appropriate lifestyle changes." He consulted my notes.

"You're a research fellow at the University of London. May I ask in what area?"

"I assist Professor Rogerson at the Institute of Historical Research. We're—" I broke off, my mouth open, "Oh."

Mathers brightened up appreciably. "Oh, indeed. Unfortunately, old chap, historians are four times more likely to suffer from T-P than the general population. Current thinking is that, being better informed, you're more susceptible to historical 'what if', ah, *imagineering*."

At least he hadn't called it "flights of fancy," but still my face burned with embarrassment. "I don't see how that could have happened. I don't use the damn thing personally. I just analyse transcripts provided by the lip-readers."

"Being within a hundred yards is enough in some cases, I'm afraid." The doctor turned to his desk and began scribbling on a pad, "I'm prescribing something for the anxiety and signing you off for an initial four weeks. This comes under the heading of an industrial injury, and your academic work simply has to take a back seat where your health is concerned, understand?"

"Yes, but—"

"But nothing. The HSE will come down like the proverbial ton of bricks on your department if the University lets you stay on. I'm afraid your esteemed Professor Rogerson will have to employ a temporary replacement or find something else to occupy his time for the next month or so." He tapped the pen on his lower lip.

"Now, the most effective protection against this form of radiation is a foil-lined skullcap or wig. Any decent milliner will carry a range of approved headgear, and they'll be a damn sight better quality than those provided by the NHS."

"That's it? That's all I have to do? Hide away for a few weeks and then wear an expensive foil hat?"

He handed me the prescription. "Pretty much. As I said, it's a relatively mild condition and easily treated. I'll see you again in about a month's time, but that should be a mere formality."

I stood and nodded. "Thank you, Doctor. You've taken a great load off my mind."

"Don't mention it, and I hope you can enjoy the weekend." Mathers smiled, "Take care."

In the end it had all sounded so matter-of-fact, so trivial, but I was in a daze. The short distance between the consulting room and waiting area simply failed to register. I found myself standing at the desk with the pretty brunette receptionist looking up at me expectantly. "Yes, Mister Banks?"

My mind stubbornly remained in neutral, and I turned away with a shake of the head. The great outdoors suddenly seemed a harsh and frightening place; people would know, they would stop and point, they would laugh. I stared at the double glass doors, breathing heavily.

The receptionist laid her hand on my shoulder, making me start. "Are you all right, sir? Would you like me to call you a cab?"

I forced my mouth into the semblance of a smile. "No, no, that's quite all right, but thanks anyway. I'll walk, I need some fresh air."

She sounded concerned. "Well, if you're quite—"

But I was gone, preferring potential ridicule to certain sympathy. I wandered aimlessly, shoulders hunched against the catcalls that never came. There was a pharmacy ahead, and I fumbled in my jacket pocket for the wadded-up prescription. My fingers closed instead around a thin, oblong shape. It was a business card, on good-quality stock, for "The Belmarsh Foundation," with an address in Earlsfield but no telephone number. On the reverse was a handwritten "8:30pm" and beneath that, "Answers."

Answers? I wasn't even sure I understood the questions.

...

Earlsfield, SW18, 8:26 pm

Despite the grandiose title, The Belmarsh Foundation turned out to be the bottom half of a partitioned terraced house in Duntshill Road, not far from the station. I watched from across the street, in the shadow of a stunted elm. There were no signs of life. The hallway behind the frosted glass fanlight was in darkness, and heavy-duty Venetian blinds covered the bay window.

I couldn't hang about indefinitely, as someone was bound to call the police and report me for loitering, with or without intent. So, I crossed the empty roadway and raised my hand to knock on the front door.

It opened, taking me by surprise. The surgery receptionist stood there—the brunette— only now she had close-cropped hair. I lowered my awkward fist, at a loss for words. She half-smiled and stood to the side.

"Welcome, John, I'm so glad you could make it. I'm Hazel, by the way. Go down the hallway to the kitchen, then straight through to the conservatory. The others are already here."

I hesitated. "Others? Look, what's all this about?"

"It may help to think of Belmarsh as a place where we discuss alternatives, but, please, this isn't a conversation for the doorstep."

I squeezed past her and walked down the narrow hall, noting a foil-lined hat and wig hanging on the coat rack. The white-tiled kitchen was cold and lacked the usual dirty dishes, cereal boxes, and other clutter normally associated with a living household. I moved on, conscious of Hazel's footsteps close behind. The conservatory was a modern extension sandwiched between the adjacent houses, with only the rear wall offering any view of the narrow garden. Despite the background burble of central heating, there was a damp chill to the air. It was obvious that the Belmarsh "alternatives" weren't discussed very often.

Two men sat there, waiting. The younger appeared nervous, restless, half-rising as I entered, only to flop down again when his companion didn't stir. This second man was middle-aged with short grey hair, moustache, and goatee. He seemed to be mounting a one-man Edwardian revival, right down to the silver-topped cane and black Homburg resting on the side-table.

Hazel stood beside me. "John, this is Richard. . . " (hesitant smile) ". . . and Leon" (no reaction). "Please, take a seat."

The four chairs in the room were arranged in a rough diamond pattern, facing inwards. Leon toyed with his cane. "You have taken your first *small step* towards the truth, John Banks." I jerked, as if touched by a live wire, and that earned me a thin-lipped smile, "Congratulations." He had an accent, an odd inflection, but nothing I could pin down.

I sat there, floundering for a reply, but Hazel came to my rescue. "Leon, don't tease the poor man. You know how fragile someone in his condition can be."

Leon inclined his head. "As you wish, Fraulein. Well, John, we both have an interest in Apollo Eleven, do we not?"

"Ah, yes, well, I guess you could say that."

"Armstrong and Aldrin, such a tragic loss. Nixon vowed their sacrifice would not be in vain and committed America to establishing Eagle Base as a permanent habitat on the Moon. Since then they have spent billions, trillions, of dollars keeping it manned and operational, to no appreciable scientific or military benefit. The effect of this distortion on the American economy is felt around the globe. However, no subsequent President has dared to dishonour the dead by pulling the plug, as the saying goes. Yes?"

The pain, which I'd almost gotten used to, stepped up a notch. I rubbed my temple. "Yes?"

"No." Leon sighed, "The *success* of Apollo Eleven spawned several follow-up missions, but the great American public rapidly lost interest, and the program was ultimately cancelled. No one has set foot on the Moon in over forty years."

"I don't understand. Which version is true?"

"You have a memory in your head like a cancer. A memory that is at odds with everything else you remember. A memory that is at odds with what everyone *else* remembers." He spread his hands to encompass the room, "Except us. For if not friends, then we are at least fellow sufferers."

I shook my head as if that would somehow dislodge the false past. "No, *no*. How can we all be having the same hallucination? I'm ill, that's all, ill, a recognised condition. This is just a cruel trick."

"Humanity is at war, Herr Banks." Leon tapped his own temple with the head of the cane, "Both up here and in the wide world. Against who or what I cannot say, but our past is being altered in an attempt to manipulate the future. Fortunately our adversary can only take a broad-brush approach, changing major events. We, on the other hand, are a guerrilla band, able to pick at loose threads until the entire tapestry of lies unravels."

"God, Leon, you do go on sometimes." Hazel sounded both amused and irritated, "Richard, will you explain? In English, please."

The younger man leaned forward in his chair. "The chronoscope is our window on the past but we have to make damn sure its presence goes undetected. If our digital camouflage isn't primo, then the link won't open. It won't open, because there's no recorded instance of us spying on the past." He scratched his head, "I know, I know, it's one of those causality paradoxes that will turn your mind inside-out if you think about it too much. Anyway, you *could* abandon any attempt at concealment and show someone in the past a short message instead. Just a few lines but more than enough to *completely* blow their mind."

I frowned. "But you just said that can't happen, because, ah, it never has happened."

Leon looked and sounded smug. "We believe that President Nixon will be *very* interested in what we have to say, and if there was anyone obsessed with information control, it was him."

"You're going to warn Tricky Dicky about this unknown adversary of yours? What possible good will that do? It's certainly not information he could act on without someone asking some damn awkward questions. Either that, or they'll have him committed." I blinked, "Had him committed, except that they didn't. My head hurts."

The older man just smiled. "Back in the nineteen-sixties NASA was certain a spectacular disaster before they reached the Moon would send manned space flight the way of the Zeppelin. Even a significant postponement was viewed with alarm, and given the available technology a major systems failure was always a distinct possibility. So they initiated a fall-back plan, Project Capricorn."

"Never heard of it."

"I should think not. Simply put, it allowed for the simulation of an Apollo mission, with the full co-operation of the astronauts involved, culminating in their air-drop as part of a faked re-entry sequence."

I snorted. "Bollocks. That's, like, the worst conspiracy theory I've *ever* heard of. Someone would have talked, especially after all this time."

Leon shook his head. "You are dealing with true believers here, John. Patriots prepared to sacrifice anything, *everything*, if that meant America was first to the Moon. Anyway, a Capricorn simulation was only to be contemplated in extreme circumstances."

I stood up. "I can't listen to any more of this. I may be ill, but at least I've accepted that I have a problem. You three, you're all in denial."

Hazel also stood, partially blocking my exit. "Please, John, just listen for one more minute."

I sighed and turned to face Leon directly. "So, let me guess, you're going to tell me that Apollo Eleven, *our* Apollo Eleven, was faked?"

"Oh, no, my friend, but it *could* have been."

We stared at each other for a long moment. I sucked in a deep breath. "You're going to scare Nixon, convince him to call-off the real Moon landing in favour of a damn *pageant*? Christ! How?" The penny continued to drop. "Oh, bugger off! *Me?* I've never been in the same room as a bloody chronoscope, let alone programmed one."

Richard fished a small vacuum-packed object from his pocket.

"This is a designator chip for the standard Mark Two, just like the model you have at the University." He licked his lips, "Now, it was a bit of a rush job, seeing as how Hazel didn't give us the heads-up until earlier today, but everything should work just fine. All you have to do is swop this baby for the one already in the slot, and away we go. To the observers at this end, it will look like your typical failed insight, end of story."

I glared at him.

"All I have to do? Listen, *Dick*, apart from the small fact that I don't have security clearance for the

16

operations area, I'm now also banned from the entire building on health and safety grounds. So think again."

Leon pointed at me with his cane. "Not until Monday, Herr Banks. It will take until then for the bureaucracy to act upon Mather's diagnosis. So we have a small window of opportunity, should you have the stomach for this enterprise."

"It's for all of us, John." Hazel was almost pleading, "For everyone out there who knows, deep down, that something is *wrong*."

"If I do this, what will it achieve? If the past has been corrupted, can a lie change things back?" No one answered. I held out my hand for the chip. "See, if this doesn't come off, sunshine, you best hope we don't end up sharing the same padded cell or you are *so* fucking dead."

...

The Institute staff were used to me working Saturday mornings and didn't bat an eyelid when I pitched up around ten. There were other sad-sack individuals about, as historians don't tend to have much of a life outside academia. I had no plan, not even an inkling, and already regretted the previous evening's uncharacteristic display of bravado.

I walked down to the basement, conscious of sweat tickling the small of my back. The depleted uranium used in its construction meant that the chronoscope couldn't be housed above ground, plus tucking it away down here simplified security matters. Yet there was no protection detail on duty when I reached the bottom corridor, and the double doors of the operations room stood wide open.

The terms *gift horse* and *too easy* vied for my attention.

I stepped cautiously over the threshold, expecting to be challenged at any moment. All the operators were gathered at the far end of the long room, clustered around some item of equipment giving off a flickering blue aura.

17

Nobody looked in my direction. The chronoscope squatted under the strip lights; a brooding gunmetal toad.

"It is a mere toy, of course, a trinket." Leon stood beside me. He wore a pristine lab coat and carried a heavy-duty protective visor around his neck. "Yet the technology it represents leads inexorably to time-travel."

Surprise and fear couldn't agree amongst themselves, and so my mind opted for dull-witted acceptance instead.

"Leon? But if you have access, if you work here, then why give me the chip? Why not do this yourself?"

"Because I cannot change anything, Herr Banks. Not here, not now." He straightened his tie. "And I am out of time."

"Doctor Prinz? Sir?" One of the technicians called from across the room. He ignored me, so perhaps I was accepted as an assistant or similar lackey.

Prinz settled his visor in place. "You must excuse me, but they require adult supervision, as the saying goes." He walked over and was absorbed into the huddle. No one paid me any further attention.

I stepped up to the helpfully labelled "Targeting Array." The Eject button did just that, and I swopped my chip for the one currently in place. A red light went green. I turned on my heel and left, without breaking into a run.

...

The wall clock in my office crawled towards 11 am, the time of the next scheduled insight. I could have run away, I suppose, but I found being surrounded by my books and papers more comforting than the thought of skulking in some alleyway. Anyway, if anything went wrong there would be no place to hide.

10:59

11:00

11:01

My background headache vanished, the sudden absence of pain making me gasp. For a moment the room

18

around me seemed unfamiliar, but the feeling faded like the memory of an interrupted dream. I blinked and rubbed my eyes. Everything appeared as it should, apart from the desk calendar, which still showed Friday. I tore off the top sheet—and laughed, staring at the daily quotation for Saturday, July 21.

One giant leap for mankind.

About the Author

Martin Clark is a freelance writer and occasional poet.

He is the author of supernatural noir novellas formally produced by Eggplant Literary Productions (now sadly defunct) now taken on by Tickety Boo Press, and short stories in recent Third Flatiron anthologies. He also contributes to several online publications including Mythaxis.co.uk, Timelesstales.com, and Kraxon.com. His range of subject matter includes science fiction, urban fantasy, romance, and westerns. He puts this down to the somewhat eclectic mobile lending library where he grew up.

He works as a local government officer in south-west Scotland but still finds time to be an evil stepfather.

We've been looking forward to more stories set in the universe of Dr. Leon Prinz.

*****~~~~~*****

The Time It Happened

Lincoln's Watch

by Atar Hadari

Joe Keenan always wanted to own Abraham Lincoln's timepiece. One day, in high school, many years ago now, a teacher with a long blond pony tail held up a grainy photograph of a man in a long, black suit. Joe had thought he looked dimly familiar, and was sure that he would see him again. Then he read, in the small print under the photograph in the slippery book the teacher smiling and nodding passed their way (at least it was slippery when it got to him)—he read something was special about the watch that Lincoln wore, because it had been stolen from his pocket, sometime between when he was shot and when they laid him down again on the bed across the street from Ford's Theatre, to die. The watch had never been seen again.

When the watch, or something claiming to be the watch, came up at an auction on a commercial website, he clicked like a madman, freezing his screen twice and dropping his wallet on the floor while struggling to get his credit card out. Then he headed out of the coffee shop, taking his two carrier bags with him and wondering how he would get the money so his card would not be taken away. His car had gone with his second wife, and now he went—with his the two bags full of toothpaste, soap, and a change of clothes—from place to place, to the coffee shops at Santa Monica, to the Internet cafes to check the Lincoln auction sites, and sometimes down to the pier, where he could hide his bags behind the oil drums while he slept. Of course, the watch hadn't been on any Lincoln memorabilia site. The watch had seemed to come to him out of a site he barely visited, an open auction. The item about Lincoln's watch wasn't even highlighted. People in cyberspace don't care about history, he sighed, highlighting the list of celebrity timepieces and arguing with himself whether it was worth a look—but he always did look under L. There was no L in the listing for the item, as it happened. It came up under the actual L listed items (Laroux, Liberace, Lindbergh), but there was no actual L in the name as it appeared next to the watch:

incoln, Abraham—Pocket watch, 1864 manufacturer stamp, imported by Barrault. Condition: Good as might be expected. Seller: Anonymous.

That line of description caught his eye. Good as might be expected? What did that mean? Was it working? Did somebody bang it against Booth's pistol as they dragged the chain out of Abe's coat, along with odd Presidential orders and stains of leaking pens and old ink?

As if in answer, another line or two came up on the slowly filling screen.

"Keeps time," the last line said, under the space where it had specified condition. Joe Keenan used the last credit on his Amex card that he got when he was a student and had kept even though his job went, the condo went, and all the other cards went before Cindy finally left. Cindy never really had understood about time, or what a watch could mean to a man who had never known what he was meant to be waiting for, through hours staring at the clock on the wall for whatever to end.

She was a tall girl, had been skinny when he met her in high school but filled out slowly into a long, broad ripple of shaking blond hair by the time he married her right before college. She was a woman always in a hurry and loved to rush. Joe waited for things, for jobs to end, for days to pass. And so the jobs did end, inevitably. And finally his will to try them ended just before Cindy's will to see his face in the morning faded away. She said, "What are you waiting for, Joe?" And he had to say that he couldn't say.

He gave the address of the Y where he had last stayed. They kept mail there for three weeks before throwing it out. He had never lost a postcard sent to him at the Y. He even got a Christmas card from Cindy there, a year or two back. He never answered. When she left, she said, "I can't wait, Joe. Whatever it is, I hope it comes to you." She took the car. He packed her things, what she had left. And then he sat at home without a job waiting for her to come pick up what she forgot. She came one day while he was out getting the groceries with food stamps, and left a postcard of Ford's Theatre with her forwarding address on it. That was why, when she wrote to him again, on the same photo card, he threw the crumpled thing away. The past and the present don't mix, except in daydreams.

He went every day to look for the parcel containing the watch he had ordered at auction. They got to telling him, "Joe, it ain't here yet. Give it a break. Try us next week. Even UPS takes a while."

But he went every day. After a week his best buddy there, Mario, the Greek with the split upper lip and tattoo of the Johnny Reb flag on his left arm, said, "You got to stop bothering the caretakers, Joe, or they'll stamp on your parcel on principle when it shows up." Joe nodded but couldn't do it. The best he could do was wait for twilight before coming around to call and ask for his parcel, right around the time when the shifts changed. And it was at that hour one day that Melanie had his parcel.

Melanie was a former Canadian waitress who drifted down from Vancouver, where the acting was not as easy to get into as they said, and she had stayed in L.A. She was a short girl with freckles on her nose and eyes that got lost beneath ginger hair. She threw the parcel at him when he came to the counter, not looking to see whether he caught the small brown, scuffed thing or not. "There y'go, ya happy?" she said.

"Ecstatic," Joe breathed. It was a box, three inches wide by four inches long, with worn brown velvet and grey on the outside. The watch was steel or brass, a pale yellow—the kind of yellow a urine sample would be if you hadn't eaten lately—and Joe knew about those. He took the watch out of the box. The white clock face snapped open at him. It said twenty to one.

"Got the time, Melanie?" he said, back at the counter.

"Not even if you have the inclination," she said. "It's seven thirty."

"This watch is slow," Joe Keenan said in mixed wonder and disgust.

"Maybe it's fast, and you don't know it," Melanie smiled, under the fringe. "Stick around, maybe it'll tell the right time at midnight."

"I don't have that long," Joe Keenan said. He went out where the early moon was sallow. The wan light shone on the watch face. Joe listened to the mechanism. It hissed and spun beneath his ear.

"Joe." Melanie was standing at the open back door of the Y, looking out into the parking lot. "Have you thought you might ask for your money back on that thing? I'm sure you can't spare it."

"Do I look like this doesn't matter to me?"

"No," Melanie replied, flicking back her hair, "I just. . . Joe, what is a watch that you so—like—wanted, if it doesn't keep time?"

"It's five hours now, until one," Joe said. The watch said one, and a minute. "I always knew whoever got this watch off Lincoln's body must have been a cold, heartless son of a bitch," Joe said, "I mean, couldn't they wait till he'd died, even?"

"Apart from that, Mrs. Lincoln," Melanie said, "What did you think of the show?" And she mimed a gun and cocked a trigger, before making a cough of a fired shot connecting and throwing her head to one side.

"You could love this watch," Joe said. "I can see why somebody must have felt they had to take it from him."

...

At midnight, under the pier, Joe Keenan dug the watch out of his chest (he had buried it under his shirt in case of robbery) and exposed it to the light. The boardwalk neon and the streetlights from the First Avenue promenade were faint, but he could make out the face by the moonlight, which reflected off the dial's white face. It still said one. The clock whirred, and its little engine wheezed like a thing that knew no rest, but the hour hand still said one—now it was twenty to one again—though Joe knew the time was twelve from the digital sign on the boardwalk. The hour hand swayed, but it always came to one again. Joe Keenan sighed. What did it mean? He searched his bags. Somewhere in there he'd printed out the watch description. "Keeps perfect time," the ad now read. He could have sworn it had just said "Keeps time," before, on the cool glass screen.

Two policemen came along the sand. Joe turned to one. "Excuse me sir," he said, "You couldn't tell me what time Lincoln died?"

"Funny you should ask," the other one said. He had a nightstick and an orange traffic cop's jacket across his sturdy middle. "John Wilkes Booth shot him about twenty minutes into the first act, but the play had been delayed for him to arrive. I believe he was shot around nine o'clock. Right around now, actually, Pacific time. And I believe, sir, I will have to ask you to clear the beach."

"Do you believe your job is a fair use of your time?" Joe Keenan asked the cop.

"I believe in civic duty," the other cop said. "Are you resisting an officer in the execution of his duties, scumbag?"

"I just wanted to see what time this watch will say in a minute," Joe said.

"Lincoln was actually carried away from the theatre," the first cop said, taking out the nightstick from

25

his belt, "And died in the house across the street about an hour after he was shot. But he was real strong. Are you strong, scumbag?"

"I used to bench press," Joe said.

"You hear that Archie?" the first cop said, "This guy's hands are lethal weapons. I believe use of all necessary force is justified by the manual."

"Are you fucking with me?" the cop in the orange jacket said. "Why you wanna know about Lincoln? What? You think it's funny? The guys downtown told you I used to teach history high school? What? You think it's funny they closed down the high school in my home town and I got laid off? You think it's funny they shot a special man?"

"I always wanted to know what it felt like to be near this watch," Joe Keenan said, and then he felt the cosh connect against his temple and the knee come up into his stomach, but not the gun, which was the last to come out and be pressed against the back of his neck as he retched from being kicked. He couldn't see which one of the policemen held it, because his face was in the sand. He held the watch out, and it was cold and lovely in his hand. The pearls he had bought Cindy with the first real check he got out of that job had been cold, white and small as shark's teeth. She had worn them driving away and shaking her head, shaking that fringe out of her eyes. The watch was so cool in his hand, he could have sworn it was like nobody really held it. Like it was unaware of anything or anyone. Just ticking away like an ambition, a will to something you could never find. Or never hold for too long.

A shot rang over the pier. The cops filing the homicide report described a tall man dressed in black running away along the beach. They said they stopped to check Joe's vital signs, and the suspect faded into the dark. Joe Keenan's watch, as he died, said twenty to one again. On the boardwalk, the face of the digital display clicked onto twelve forty, just as Joe was wheeled into the ambulance on the gurney and dropped the watch into the waiting sand.

The doors of the ambulance closed once, opened, then closed again for good. One of the cops, the one who'd known the hour of Lincoln's death, looked at the watch fall into the sand, said, "Wiseass," and turned back toward the sea, kicking sand up over the white face as he walked on toward the comforting sound of waves hitting the breakers and falling back.

About the Author

Atar Hadari was born in Israel, raised in England, and studied poetry and playwrighting with Derek Walcott at Boston University. His plays have won awards from the BBC, Arts Council of England, National Foundation of Jewish Culture (New York), European Association of Jewish Culture (Brussels), and the Royal Shakespeare Company, where he was Young Writer in Residence. Plays have been staged at the Finborough Theatre, Wimbledon Studio Theatre, Chichester Festival Theatre, the Mark Taper Forum (where he was a Mentor Playwright), Nat Horne Studio Theatre (New York) and in Valdez, Alaska. His "Songs from Bialik: Selected Poems of H. N. Bialik" (Syracuse University Press) was a finalist for the American Literary Translators' Association Award, and his poems have won the Daniel Varoujan award from New England Poetry Club, the Petra Kenney award, a Paumanok poetry award, and many other prizes. His debut poetry collection, "Rembrandt's Bible," was recently published by Indigo Dreams Press, and his "Lives of the Dead: Poems of Hanoch Levin" is forthcoming from Arc Publications. Recently awarded the first British Centre for Literary Translation's Mentorship in Hebrew, he is

The Time It Happened

currently translating the classic Hebrew novel by Chaim Hazaz, "The Gallows" with Nicholas de Lange.

*****~~~~~*****

Going Viral

by Dan Koboldt

Our laboratory was on the verge of closing when we got the virus.

It came in a sturdy Styrofoam cooler. I noticed it, because of the international mail coupons, and the stamp from U.S. Customs: NOT INSPECTED. I didn't blame them. Most people didn't want a closer look at virus samples from the Third World. To be honest, I was a bit reluctant to open the box myself.

I'd just worked up the courage, when Finch walked in. In the two years he'd been my mentor, he always wore the same things: shapeless khakis, an ancient button-down shirt, and convex glasses that lent him a sort of bug-eyed appearance. And the comb-over, let's not forget that.

"Morning, Sam," he called.

"Morning, Ray," I said. "Just got a new bug from Argentina."

"What kind?" he asked.

I plucked the small plastic tube from a bed of dry ice and shook it off. "Adenovirus, T1."

"Sounds promising!" he said. He always said that, and he'd been wrong every time.

Raymond Finch had been on the fringe of greatness for decades. I can't even remember how far down on my list he was when I sent out my postdoc applications. But I'd gone to the interview and really liked him. He was more human and less shark than most research scientists.

Then again, that might be why the lab's funding had about dried up.

"There's a seminar in the library," Finch said.

I managed not to groan. "What's the topic?"

"Cell division timing. Any interest?"

"No, I'd better start running this one," I said.

Frankly speaking, I didn't want to face the other professors and postdocs. Rumors about our lab closing were making the rounds. Even the grad students were looking at me with a mixture of pity and disdain. I'd rather spend my time with a Third World virus. That's how bad it was.

"Be careful. Silva's found some really odd viruses down there," Finch said. He topped off his coffee and left. It was probably for the best. Being around him made me a little angry sometimes, because of the funding stuff, even though I owed him a lot.

I put the tube in the centrifuge and then pipetted a couple of microliters into a cell plate. We were screening viruses for gene therapy. The more infectious, the better, as long as I didn't accidentally stab myself with the micropipette. I didn't want to get my hopes up, but we really needed a win.

Half an hour later, I checked the plate and found it empty.

"Shit," I said.

The cells were gone. Wiped out, every one of them. Which had never happened before, and really shouldn't be possible. These weren't everyday cell cultures. They were fibroblast cell lines. Skin cells, genetically altered by a retrovirus to grow indefinitely. You could even hit them with radiation and they'd survive. We called them *immortal* for a reason.

Yet this new virus had killed them, in the time it took me to eat a peanut butter and jelly sandwich.

I figured I must have screwed something up, so I pulled a fresh cell plate from inventory and ran it again. This time I put a camera on it. I came back in fifteen minutes, and the plate was empty. Again.

"You've got to be kidding me," I said.

Finch returned and refilled his mug. I swear, the man had more coffee than blood in his veins. "You missed a good one," he said.

"So did you," I said. "Watch this."

I pulled up the video on my laptop and hit Play. There was my gloved hand, pipetting the virus into the cell plate. Nothing happened for a few seconds. Then the cells nearest the entry point popped like soap bubbles. The virions were too small to see, but the effect wasn't. It was the laboratory equivalent of a bomb going off.

"What was that, bleach?" Finch asked. Not a bad question. Liquid chlorine kills almost anything.

"No. It's the new sample. Adenovirus, T1," I said.

"Now *that* is interesting."

For the first time in a long while, I had to agree.

…

It was three days later, and I'd hardly slept. We'd tried T1 on every cancer cell line in the department. It wiped out glioblastoma, melanoma, and leukemia. Even the fabled HeLa cell line, the one notoriously taken from Henrietta Lacks. HeLa cells grew so fast, they were like an infectious agent themselves. The new virus cut through them like a knife.

Strangely, when we infected normal tissue cultures, the virus had no effect. But T1 killed any cancer cell within reach. Finch brought in a few of the other faculty members to watch. None of them had visited our lab in months; I guess the smell of failure was too strong. They were eager now, though.

Finch was, too. I came in one morning and found him at the bench, in his ancient lab coat, running more tests.

"Ray?" I asked.

He looked at me with red-rimmed eyes. "Hey, Sam," he said.

"It's eight in the morning."

"Wow. Really?"

"Were you here all night?" I asked, though I knew the answer. He looked like hell.

"I think we've really got something."

"What's next?" I asked.

"Animal models. And then clinical trials." He sighed. "We don't have the resources for either, I'm afraid."

"The university has deep pockets," I said. "Maybe the chancellor would—"

But Finch was already shaking his head. "The university's also very big. And the chancellor doesn't even know who I am."

"Where's his office?" I asked.

"The South Building," Finch said. "Behind about ten secretaries who also don't know me."

"Yeah, but what floor?"

"The thirty-second, I believe."

Formulas whirred in my head, estimating speed and the number of stops between. "That gives us about a hundred and eighteen seconds."

"For what?" he asked.

"To sell the chancellor on funding T1."

…

We sprang our ambush on Thursday morning. Finch practiced his pitch three times to work out the stutters. I was nervous, too, but I tried not to show it. I needed him confident.

We loitered in the lobby of the South Building, trying to appear casual. At five minutes to eight, the chancellor swept by with a couple of staffers in tow.

"Here we go," Finch said.

"Game time," I said.

A small crowd formed by the elevator doors. At least one other faculty member had had the same idea.

We hadn't counted on vying with someone else for the chancellor's attention, damn it. Pitching T1 in two minutes would be hard enough as it was.

The elevator dinged. I moved into position by the interloping researcher, a balding, middle-aged fellow in a stained lab coat. He had a cup of coffee in hand. No lid. Perfect. I staged a violent sneeze, knocking the man's coffee all over him.

"Jesus!" he shouted. His eyes were murderous.

"Oh my God, I'm so sorry!" I said.

He stood there, fuming, dripping onto the tile floor. Meanwhile, the elevator doors opened just long enough to swallow the chancellor, his staffers, and Finch.

"Come on, I'll buy you another cup," I said.

I walked with him over to the coffee shop. I caught a glimpse of his ID badge.

"You're from Radiology?" I asked.

"Yes," he said. "Randy Masset."

"I'm Sam Ellison," I said. "I'm over in Virology with Raymond Finch."

He grunted. "Never heard of him."

"I think that might change," I said.

Randy was a nice guy, as it turned out. His grant renewal had just been denied by the National Institutes of Health. I felt bad for him, because I'd been there. Things were tough all over. He let me buy him coffee, and headed back to his lab to change.

I got a cup for myself and checked my watch. Riding up and down should have taken about five minutes. Where was Finch?

Another hour later he strolled out of the elevator. He saw me and grinned. "We've got our funding!"

...

I'll never forget T1's first clinical trial, a last-hope sort of thing for advanced pancreatic cancer. Finch and I were worried sick. What if T1 had some side effect we hadn't foreseen? What if some of the patients died? We'd feel terrible if something happened. We were virologists; we didn't usually hold people's lives in our hands.

The other treatment in the trial was called Halmatinib. It had *millions* of dollars behind it. Bottom line, we didn't like our chances.

Those two weeks, waiting for the first patient follow-up, were torture. Finally Finch's office phone rang. I watched him through the glass as he answered, listened for a minute, and then hung up. I hurried around to his door.

"Well?" I asked. I knew I sounded rude, but I couldn't help it.

"The Halmatinib patients aren't responding," he said. "They're actually doing worse than the placebo group. Some kind of toxicity."

"What about ours?" I asked.

"Complete remission."

"What?"

"The tumors are gone," he said. He looked like he hardly believed it himself.

I shook my head. "Holy *shit*, Ray!"

It only took a day for the results to leak out. I guess end-stage cancer patients and their families are a tight-knit group. A mob of them marched on the treatment ward, chanting "Give T1 to everyone!"

We had enough data by then, so the university gave out the rest of the trial supply of T1. Within a week, every single test patient was cancer-free. Adenovirus T1 got fast-tracked FDA approval after that. Halmatinib was quietly repurposed as a pesticide.

. . .

When our paper came out, Dr. Finch went from near obscurity to international fame. Calls and e-mails flooded in. I didn't mind—I actually enjoyed the attention, if I'm being honest—but it took a toll on Dr. Finch. I hadn't realized just how much, until the morning he collapsed in the lab. Must have been all the stress.

34

"How about keeping to your office for a while?" I suggested. "I can unplug the phone and set an auto-responder on our e-mail accounts."

Finch didn't protest, so I did both. I closed his office door and positioned myself outside. If anyone wanted to talk to us, they'd have to do so in person.

I honestly didn't expect anyone would go that far.

…

A man waited in the hallway when I got to work the next morning. He had to be private sector. Anyone wearing a suit in our poorly lit hallways stuck out like a game show host in the unemployment line.

"Good morning," he said. He smiled, flashing white teeth.

"Uh, hello," I said, distracted. I'd just realized I was wearing two different shoes.

"You must be Sam Ellison." He pressed my hand in a firm handshake. He had dark hair and a faint accent, maybe British colonial.

"Yes. Can I help you?" I asked.

"Is Dr. Finch around?"

"No. Why?" I asked.

"I've got a proposition for him."

"I don't think we're interested," I said. I got the lab's door open and flipped on the lights.

He laughed and followed me in. "What, you don't want to make six figures?"

"That's not really our thing," I said.

"Do me a favor. Look out the window," he said.

I obliged him and looked down at the parking lot next to our ramshackle building. Among the sedans and mopeds and beat-up minivans was a bright red vehicle. Like, a racecar. "Whoa!" I said. "What is that, a Ferrari?"

"It's a Lamborghini," he said, as if speaking to a child. "Five hundred horsepower. That's the kind of lifestyle we're offering you and Dr. Finch."

He wasn't at the window, so I had to ask him. "Did you park in a handicapped spot?"

"I might have." He frowned. "Why?"

"Because it's being towed."

He cursed and ran out. I shook my head. If he'd wanted to impress me, he should have brought a Tesla.

...

I had the lab to myself for half an hour before I caught the first whiff of perfume. It was faint but alluring, scented like rose petals and morning dew. I looked up from the microscope and saw a girl in the doorway. Black skirt, white blouse, blonde hair. And *gorgeous*. I felt my mouth drop open, but I couldn't close it. She wore a lab coat, too, though I doubted it belonged to her.

"Hello, Sam," she said. Her voice was soft but sultry; it made my spine tingle.

"Hello," I said. "I'm— I'm Sam."

A distant part of my brain was aware that she knew that already, but her looks and voice and perfume had made everything cloudy.

"Sam Ellison," she said. She smiled a little, bit her lip. "Discoverer of adenovirus T1."

Co-discoverer would be more accurate. "That's right," I said.

"I'm Shannon," she said.

I stood, uncomfortably aware of my shaggy appearance. "Nice to meet you," I said.

"I would love to hear about it sometime," she said.

"Well, I would love to tell it."

She glided closer to me. "How about lunch?"

"Sure!" I said. I sounded like a little kid being asked to go to the zoo.

"Maybe I could say hello to Dr. Finch." She reached for his door, and it broke the spell.

"No!" I shouted. "I mean, Dr. Finch isn't taking visitors right now."

She pouted. "Even for a few minutes?"

I almost said yes. I really wanted to, but I couldn't let the floodgates open. "I'm sorry," I said.

She made a disgusted sound in her throat and stormed out, tossing the lab coat to the floor as she left.

"Are we still on for lunch?" I called.

No answer.

I sighed. "Guess I'm back to peanut butter and jelly."

...

I finally had a quiet afternoon and tried to catch up on e-mail. Messages were flooding in from all over the globe—congratulations, for the most part. Invitations to collaborate. Even a few more personal and risqué offers. Of course, I was looking at one of these when the cowboy showed up.

"Reckon you're that Ellison fella," he said.

His voice startled me. He wore a light linen suit, dark tie, and a tan Stetson hat. He strolled in without waiting to be invited. I really had to start locking the lab door.

"Sam Ellison, yes," I said.

"Name's Ralph Munroe," he said. "Pork Farmers Alliance."

"You mean, like, pigs?" I asked.

"That's right. But call 'em hogs, for the most part."

"Okay," I said. "How can I help you?"

"It's a fine thing you've done with that adenovirus," he said. He drawled out every syllable in the word. *Uh-denn-oh-viirus.*

"Uh, thanks."

"Have you thought about a delivery vehicle?"

"I—" It took me a moment to realize he'd really asked about that. "Yeah. We've been kicking around some ideas." T1 was so infectious, we had a lot of options for giving it to patients. An oral vaccine was the leading contender.

"Mind if I float one your way?"

37

"Sure."

"Bacon."

I stared at him for a moment. "I'm sorry, did you say *bacon?*"

"People love bacon," he said.

"Well, yeah, but I'm not sure that it's the healthiest—"

"Listen, son," he said. He stepped close enough to put a meaty hand on my shoulder. "Got to be honest with you. The pork industry's hurting right now. Cost of feed keeps going up, and this turkey bacon is killing us."

"I kind of like turkey bacon," I said.

"It's unnatural!" he said. "Tastes like cardboard, if you ask me."

"Well, we're still looking at a lot of options," I said.

"Mind if I have a word with Dr. Finch?"

"He's not in today," I lied.

He looked at me, working the toothpick in his mouth. I felt like he knew I wasn't being honest. "All right, son. Here's my card." He handed it to me and sauntered out.

I heard scuffling noises in the hallway. Grunting, curses. Six seconds later another cowboy sauntered in, a different guy in a dark Stetson. No toothpick. His powder-blue linen suit looked a little disheveled. "Hey there," he said.

"Hello," I said.

He grinned like nothing was wrong, and came over to shake my hand. "Billy McIntyre. Turkey Farmers of America."

...

The parade continued for weeks. Politicians and palm-pressers showed up; they wanted the strain named after them. Oh, the promises they made! Grant funding, tax exemptions. Buildings with our names on them. I nearly caved a few times. But I let no one through. Finch's

38

door remained closed, with only a faint hum coming from behind it.

Meanwhile, adenovirus T1 took the medical community by storm. Cancer patients were going into remission all over the world. We knew that tumors evolved, especially in the face of treatment, but none withstood T1. It evolved faster. We had no idea how it killed only cancerous cells without harming the patient; that would be the subject of study for decades to come. But it worked, and it worked so well that every pharmaceutical company agreed to a non-exclusive license. This was the end of cancer therapy; they couldn't afford to miss out. With so large a supply, anyone who needed T1 could get it.

It was only a matter of time until the letter came from Stockholm. Finch was up for the Nobel Prize. I thought his chances were good, though the final decision wouldn't be made until October. I kept everyone at bay while the weeks passed. I answered his e-mails and took his messages, handled the paperwork for the lab.

"Dr. Finch is too busy," I said to those who called. The chancellor had insisted we plug our phones back in. "I'm happy to pass along your message to him."

I let no calls through. I blocked every visitor. The waiting for good news seemed never to end.

...

The first of October, a messenger knocked on the lab door. He was a young guy, clean-shaven and looking bored. "Raymond Finch?" he asked.

"This is his lab," I answered.

"I've got a letter for him. Certified mail."

My heart rate quickened. "Is it from Sweden?" I asked.

He glanced at it and furrowed his brow. "How'd you know?"

"I'll sign for it," I said.

I took the letter and sent him away, then closed the door to the hallway. Locked it, too; I'd learned my lesson. I ripped open the letter and skimmed it, hardly breathing.

"Yes!" I shouted.

I ran in to see Finch. His dusty office was still and quiet, but for the whir of the minus 80 degree freezer. I switched it off and lifted the lid.

"Good news, Ray," I said. "We did it."

For a moment it seemed that he smiled, but I knew it was my imagination. Those blue lips hadn't moved for months. After he'd collapsed, I'd felt his pulse weaken, and then fade. Heart attack. Nothing I could do. But you had to be alive to win the Nobel Prize, and I didn't want to win it without him.

Once he was nice and thawed out, I picked up the phone and called 9-1-1.

###

About the Author

Dan Koboldt has worked as a genetics researcher for over a decade. He also writes speculative fiction (sci-fi/fantasy), and is represented by Jennie Goloboy of Red Sofa Literary Agency. He lives with his wife and three children in St. Louis, Missouri.

*****~~~~~*****

Stilled Life

by Ellen Denton

All over the city, people stopped in their tracks, and wide-eyed, disbelieving faces turned upward to the sky. Had anyone spoken to anyone else at that moment, they would have been stunned to know that no two people were seeing the same thing.

Mrs. Louisa Figlia, a 62-year-old widow, dropped to the concrete pavement and made the sign of the cross over her chest. She didn't notice that she'd fallen on a piece of broken glass and cut her knee. For now, all her attention was riveted onto the radiant, golden image of Jesus on a crucifix hovering in the sky above her. The glow he emitted made the raindrops all around him shine with inner light.

Jimmy Connelly, a shy, lonely, five year old, almost cried when he saw Snow White, looking exactly like she did when he saw her at Disneyland, slowly descend with a puppy in her arms and hand it to him. As she rose back into the sky, he saw the seven dwarfs marching upward with her on a path made from a rainbow. Doc led them, beating a drum, followed by a widely grinning Happy, who waved a baton. The last thing he heard, after the drumbeats faded into the distance, was a barely audible sneeze.

Carl Mitchell, a ruthless corporate raider, had just stepped out of a downtown high-rise and was about to open his umbrella, but stopped when he saw raindrops coalesce into watery rectangles midair and shimmer into thousand dollar bills. They wafted *en masse* to the ground and skittered around his feet like autumn leaves in the wind.

He glanced around at the other people standing on the sidewalk looking up or who had pulled their cars over to crane their necks and see the sky through their rainy windshields. No one else seemed to notice the bills piling up in wind-swept drifts around the sidewalk.

He pinched himself to make sure he wasn't dreaming, then got down on his knees and gathered them up handfuls at a time, stuffing them down his shirt, pants, boxer shorts, and into every pocket. He crawled along the ground around people's legs, careful not to disturb anyone when he lifted a bill off someone's shoe.

At a shellfish stall in a mid-town farmer's market, Rico Juarez was busy tying down kiosk flaps to keep the blowing rain from spattering his merchandise. He glanced around, expecting to see people racing through the aisles with newspapers or umbrellas over their heads to get to someplace dry, but everyone stood still with their eyes raised towards the sky, the rain and wind whipping their clothes and hair.

He stepped outside of his kiosk to see what was going on, but when he looked up, saw only rain and roiling gray clouds. Puzzled, he looked around at the upward-staring crowd, when a small object rained down right beside him and splashed into a puddle. It submerged and then bounced to the surface. It was an oyster, not an Almaco Jack or Rainbow Runner food oyster, but a Tahitian black lip, the kind his father, an expert on shellfish, told him about that produced magnificent black pearls. He picked it up and moved back under the shelter of his kiosk. The creature sat in the palm of his hand, and as though by magic, the top of the shell slowly opened, revealing the most beautiful pearl Rico had ever seen.

He gently closed the shell, and after wrapping it up well in wax paper and placing it in the cash bag he wore around his waist, stepped back out into the rain and looked up again eagerly. He wondered if any more Tahitian blacks were going to be coming down.

Andrea Lane ran into a diner to get a handful of paper cups with lids. She was a single mother with no medical insurance, and one of the puddles that formed at her feet turned into the expensive insulin her diabetic son needed. She used the cups to scoop it up.

Eighty-four-year-old Elliot Levine saw his wife Elsa floating in the sky above him in a flower-print dress. She had been killed in a hit-and-run accident 17 years before. He never got to say goodbye, tell her how much he loved her, or apologize for calling her a fat-ass on the morning of her death. As she hovered above, she tilted her head to him, cupped her hand to her ear, and he said all he wanted to say.

...

Hobie Tobin had spent the last two hours grading the essays of his tenth-grade English class and was finally on the last one. He scribbled corrections and suggestions along the margins of its pages, and laid down the pen. He glanced at his watch; if he moved fast, he could catch the 4:50 express train before the rush-hour crowd hit in earnest.

He left the school and walked at a sharp pace down the empty, residential street toward the heavily trafficked boulevard and subway up ahead. By the time he got there the rain was coming down in sheets, and his umbrella was tilted forward to keep it off his face. He realized that, because of the storm, others probably had the same idea as he did—leave work early, rush to get to the subway before it got worse, and avoid the rush-hour crowds. The train was going to be packed.

What he didn't expect was the entire boulevard, as far as he could see in each direction, to be filled with people staring upwards and standing as still as statues in the rain.

He jerked his head up and saw nothing but rain-darkened sky. Puzzled, he walked up to the person closest to him—a man in a blue suit clutching a briefcase.

"Sir, excuse me. I just got here—what's everybody looking at?"

The man, rain streaming down his face and hair, his eyes unblinking, didn't move by so much as a fraction of an inch.

"Sir?" He now reached out and laid his hand firmly on the man's shoulder. Hobie may as well have been a ghost.

He moved away and walked slowly down the street, uncomprehending, looking at the cars stopped mid-street, and at the people on the sidewalk standing motionless and non-responsive. He got to the end of the block and noticed the clock face at the top of the City Central Bus Depot: 3:15. He looked at his own watch: 5:12. There was a woman next to him at the curb. He looked at her wrist and saw she was wearing a unisex Timex with a slip-on nylon strap, similar to the one he owned. He craned his neck down to look at the face of it: 3:15. He turned and walked a short ways back down the street to "Roseanne's," a diner where he sometimes picked up coffee on his way to work. There were people inside gathered at the window, motionless, gawking upward at the sky. He looked past them to the clock high up on the back wall: 3:15.

He turned again to the street and the people standing in the rain and realized they weren't merely standing there looking up. They were frozen in space and time.

...

His legs felt weak. He was nauseated and scared—more so than he could remember ever being in his life. He headed back the way he came, planning on returning to the school so he could sit down. He passed the stairs leading down into the subway station and heard footsteps racing up them. He backed up to see who or what it was. A girl, hollow-eyed and frantic-looking, stopped mid-step when she saw Hobie looking down at her. He realized he probably appeared as wide-eyed, panic-stricken, and confused as she did.

They continued staring at each other for a beat in time. She looked behind her, as though considering running back down into the subway, but instead turned to Hobie. Her voice was quivery with held-back crying.

"Do you. . . know what's going on?" She gestured vaguely in the direction of the subway below, as though she thought Hobie could see it from where he stood on the sidewalk.

"No—I'm—everyone up here is just standing still in the rain." At that moment, it stopped raining. He spun around to look at the street, as if the storm ending might have set everything back to normal.

The same people were still standing there looking up.

The girl's face was strained and white as she walked the rest of the way up the stairs. "I'm scared. Everyone is standing still down there too." She got to the top where Hobie was and began to sob.

He reached out to touch her shoulder, saw her wince, so drew his hand back. "Let me ask you something—are you wearing a watch?"

The girl wrinkled her brow and looked at him suspiciously. "Yes. Why?"

"Humor me a moment. What time does your watch say? I'm Hobie Tobin, by the way, I teach at Jefferson High, a few blocks away."

The girl nodded and pushed the sleeve of her rain slicker back. "It's 5:22."

Hobie looked at his own watch. "That's what I've got too. Something really frickin' insane is going on."

. . .

On their way along the boulevard back to the school, they periodically looked at clocks in stores and watches on people's wrists, all of which read 3:15.

They now sat in the teachers' break room. Hobie made them both coffee, and they sipped it in silence for a few moments. The girl, who he learned was named Anne,

45

had been coming home from work on the train. As with all the previous station stops, when it pulled into that one, people moved toward the open doors to get off, and everyone froze at the exact same moment.

"So. . . Hobie, do you have any theories on what the hell is going on?"

"Sure! We've been invaded by aliens from outer space, or I'm dreaming, and the pretty girl sitting in front of me is only a figment of my imagination, or everything is actually completely normal out there, but you and I are dead."

Anne laughed, and then turned white. "Do you think it might be that?"

"No, no, I was just kidding. Believe me, we're not dead. There's got to be some kind of rational explanation for what's going on. You have any ideas?"

"No. I wonder what everyone was looking at, though. Even the people down in the subway—they all looked up."

"Okay, so then, we can probably assume they were seeing *something*. Whether or not that something was really there, I don't know, but. . . wait a second, another thing we don't know is how widespread this is. Come on, I have an idea."

They went up one flight of stairs to John Muller's political science classroom. There was a TV/VCR set up there. After flipping through two channels of hissing static, a rerun of the movie, "Gone with the Wind," and the rolling credits for a pre-filmed soap opera that had just gone off the air, he got to the KXML news channel, one he knew was always broadcast live.

The two news anchors, Alan Redman and his co-host July Impala, were both sitting motionless at the news desk in front of the cameras, staring upwards at something on the ceiling.

He was about to try flipping to another channel, when something dark suddenly blotted out the view of the newsroom. The room briefly appeared, then blacked out once more. Now the left side of it appeared. Someone or something was moving back and forth in front of the camera.

Both Hobie and Anne watched intently for a few moments. A person, who Hobie could tell was a UPS delivery man from his uniform, moved forward and away from the camera and walked toward the news desk and the motionless Alan and July. He poked Alan Redman on the face with his index finger as though he were a clothing store mannequin, then turned around with a confused, horrified expression on his face that, under other circumstances, might have been comical. He then stumbled off to the left and out of view of the camera, still clutching the package he had been holding as though it were the last bastion of sanity on planet Earth. He appeared for a moment from another angle when he walked in front of a different camera, then was seen no more. They heard the faint sound of a door slamming off-stage somewhere.

Hobie walked to the classroom window and looked out.

"The sun is out now. There are other people like us that this—whatever "this" is—isn't happening to. Let's go back out and find some of them."

...

Stan Corbin momentarily removed his finger from the trigger of his 416 Rigby to wipe drops of stinging sweat from his eyes. He was down on one knee in the suffocating jungle heat, never taking his eyes off the bull elephant and biding his time for just the right moment.

His finger was back on the trigger, moving gently up and down over it, almost caressing it. The creature turned, and he took the shot.

At first, he thought he must have missed, because the bull didn't move—didn't even appear to hear the shot, then it swayed, snorted, and dropped to its front knees, sending a cloud of dust, grass wisps, and bugs swirling up into the air. Stan fired a second time for good measure, and the creature fell over onto its side.

Stan stood up and smiled with satisfaction. *This is a great kill. A trophy kill.* Earlier that afternoon, after leaving the drive-through at Burger King, his wife had called him a "dickless wonder" because he didn't stand up for her, or even say a single word, when the pimply-faced teenager at the window handed her out the milkshake and made a rude, joking comment about her weight. *Let's see if she calls me dickless now, when I bring **this** baby home,* he thought. *The ivory from the tusks alone will bring in. . .*

He continued his musings while slicing off strip after strip of elephant hide with his expensive, Dymondwood big-game skinner, alternating between wiping sweat from his brow and waving away mosquitoes. He stopped at one point to turn and look into the setting sun, but at that moment, when Hobie and Anne passed him on the boulevard, he was still standing exactly where Hobie first saw him, wearing the blue suit, clutching his briefcase, and staring up unblinking at the sky.

...

In a 30,000-square-foot underground bunker, puzzled scientists, grim, frowning military bigwigs, and a president who tried to appear impassive, but who was actually scared shitless, all stood around a transparent-walled chamber, staring at an object inside of it that looked like a small metal ball on a pedestal. It was sending out crazy-jagged streaks of blue lightning in all directions. All the observers were wearing what looked like oversized motorcycle helmets.

...

"Hey! Wait up. Don't be afraid."

The boy with the bandage on his head was about to bolt over a fence that would take him into the next alley over, but now slowed down and turned to look at Anne and Hobie. He was the first moving person they'd seen in two hours of walking the city.

"I'm Hobie, and this is Anne. I know this is all probably really freaky and scary to you, like it is to us. What's your name?"

"Ryan."

"Ryan, why don't you hang out with us? We're trying to find more people—people who can walk around. We've also got some food here, if you'd like some."

The relief in the boy's eyes was visible. He walked up to them.

Anne smiled and handed him one of the sandwiches they'd gotten from a vending machine before leaving the school. "What happened to your head that it's all bandaged up like that?"

"I had an operation for an accident. Got a metal plate in my head now!" He said it with the pride only a ten year old could have over such things.

Hobie stared at Ryan. "I have one in my head also. When I was fifteen, my skull got all messed up in a car accident, so they put one in. He glanced at Anne. She nodded.

"I have one. It's a permanent titanium-based patch to cover a hole in my skull.

All three of them, even ten-year-old Ryan, now looked at each other, as they shared the same dawning realization.

. . .

"You call this cataclysm a 'mistake?' An 'accident?' And are you seriously telling me that there's no way to reverse it?"

The president was at the head of the table addressing the Chairman of the Joint Chiefs of Staff, who glanced at the Military Service Chiefs for the Army, the Navy, and the Marine Corps. The chief for the Air Force was in one of the Pentagon restrooms staring up at the ceiling, and no one knew where the Chief of the National Guard Bureau was.

Those around the table looked at one another; they still wore the oversized helmets and had been since the day that their latest "war toy" was tested for the first time. It was supposed to affect only a small, remote area in the Mojave Desert in Nevada, where a few war criminals were housed.

...

Just off the coast of China, a small fishing boat drifted in a gentle swell. The fisherman and his son stood motionless on the deck, smiling blissfully and looking up at the sky.

About the Author

Ellen Denton is a freelance writer living in the Rocky Mountains with her husband and two demons who wreak havoc and hell (the cats, not the husband). This is her second appearance in a Third Flatiron anthology.

She's been published in *Carte Blanche, T. Gene Davis, Pithy Pages, Robot and Raygun, Wicked Words, Anotherealm, Body Parts, Insight, Underground Voices, Perihelion Science Fiction, Horror Garage, SpecLit, Transformation, Horror on the Installment Plan, Bards and Sages Quarterly, Binnacle, Literary hatchet, Kid's Ark, Fiction 365, You and Me, Things Japanese, Guardian Angel Publishing, Words about Work, Greenprints, Animal Wellness, Songs of Eretz Poetry Review, Country Extra,* and *Vampires2* magazines. Appearances in anthologies include April Moon books, Spider Road Press, Gothic City Press, Suddenly Lost in Words, JaSunni Productions, Dark Moon books, Spark, Spruce Mountain Press, Publishing Syndicate, Zharmae Publishing Press, See Spot Run, and Treasures Beyond

Measure. She won an Honorable Mention in L. Ron Hubbard's Writers of the Future contest, 1st place in an *On the Premises* contest, won an Enchanted Spark contest, and an editor's choice award for *Amok* anthology.

*****~~~~*****

The Time It Happened

Kin Carriers

by Jason Lairamore

Captain Marvin Gleece squeezed the bridge of his nose and looked to the screen display from the bridge of his starship. With this last strike, this ugly business would finally come to an end.

Thank all that was good and righteous.

Before his massive warship floated the last surviving arc-habitat circling Proxima Centauri. There'd originally been ten habitats around humanity's closest neighboring star. Now, there was only one.

He pressed the button that sent the missiles burning toward their target.

Though silent, the explosion was really something. The little metal moon, with its irregular blue-tinged ice coating, blew up as if it were set to go from the inside. The uniformity of the total obliteration was mind numbing. Mere moments after the initial blinding light there was nothing but the glowing sparks of debris shooting off in all directions.

"Not a word from them," First Lieutenant Kendra Fields, his second in command, said from her position beside him on the bridge. "None of the arcs ever said a thing. It's as if they were already dead."

He glanced over at her and clenched his fingers a few times to try to relieve the knotting stress that seemed to be slowly taking over his body.

"Doesn't matter," he said. "We're done and can begin the long ride back home. You're ready to go home, aren't you?" He eyed the starburst effect of the dimming debris.

"Yes, sir," she said. "Helm, set protocol for return vector. Advise the ship of timetable."

The various coordinating officers splayed about the bridge sounded off to acknowledge the order. He couldn't help but note the hopeful resignation in their tones. Every person on this ship, from the highest ranking to the custodians and cooks, took heart that returning home would somehow make what they'd done out here feel less than what it truly had been, like somehow the atrocious acts they'd committed could be erased by nothing more than time and space.

"Take us through what's left of the debris field first," he said. "I want a closer look."

First Lieutenant Fields did her duty without a hitch. "You heard the Captain. Let's make it slow and controlled. Keep sensors amped high. I don't want any surprises."

There was a hustle of activity as the entire bridge went to work on the maneuver. Captain Gleece gave a tight smile when, after only thirty seconds, the crew had built, developed, and put into play a plan that'd do exactly what he wanted done. They were a good bunch.

Fields tugged on her earlobe to disconnect her cranio-computer from the warship network and turned to him.

"What's next, sir?" she asked.

"We need a souvenir to take home."

"Sir?"

"We don't get to forget what we did out here. Right or wrong, humanity will know."

"We've recorded everything we've done. The tapes cannot be dismissed, sir." She wasn't contesting his judgment. She was digging for more information. He smiled at her ability to modulate her tone just enough to appease his sense of egotism.

"Tapes can be edited. Haven't you ever heard the old saying, 'History is written by the victors'?"

"So you think a piece of mangled wreckage put on display will do what, exactly?"

He shook his head. "We killed our own, Fields. We killed them, simply because they not only dared but also succeeded in progressing with an outlawed scientific pathway."

A little color showed on her otherwise white cheeks. He could tell she was having a hard time holding it together. She managed to keep her voice civil, though, even if it did tremble some.

"You volunteered us for this mission, sir."

He nodded and shrugged his shoulders. He had another headache coming on.

"I volunteered us so that nobody else would have to. You can bet your very last credit on the certainty that I plan to spend the rest of my life ensuring everyone knows what we've done here. Nobody will forget. They will not sweep this under the rug. I do not want another crew of outstanding men and women to have to go through what we just did."

She stared at him for a moment. There were tears in her eyes. "Yes, sir." She saluted and turned in an about-face to stride away from the bridge.

He watched her go and rubbed at the back of his head then turned toward his own quarters. He needed something for his headache.

...

The idea and deployment of the arc-habitats had started out very simply. Build them. Fill them full of people. Then send them to Proxima Centauri, making sure to set up a proper orbit to maximize the needs of the humans and their living foodstuff. The technique had worked so wonderfully in the past. Earth had long shared its orbit with twelve little ice-covered arcs.

Proxima Centauri hadn't been so lucky. They'd broken the rules.

The sympathizers back home had called it divergent social evolution, or DSE. This DSE had occurred because of the distance between the Sun and

Proxima Centauri. Earth and the sol arcs had lost touch with their far-flung brothers on Proxima. The shared cultures between the two had changed. The souls of the men and women had altered. The humans on Proxima had become something a little different from the Earthmen.

It was inevitable, they'd said.

The masses on Earth hadn't liked it. Captain Marvin Gleece had answered their call to act.

"Sir, we've been pinged," said Communication Officer Adam Healy. They were still well out from the debris field, but that shouldn't have mattered. There was nothing to ping them out here, not unless a UFO had conveniently shown up to announce that there was, in fact, intelligent life other than human beings.

Before Captain Gleece could ask for verity, one of the Radar Officers chimed in.

"We have an incoming unidentified heading straight at us. It's coming from the center of the debris field."

"Guns at the ready," Gleece said. "Give me eyes on this thing." Could the racket they'd been making really have attracted the attention of something unknown?

The screen display came online to show what looked like a rough, pitted circle with various bits of gadgetry poking out of it. There was more than one strobe light flashing a multitude of colors. He shook his head. The word, 'PEACE' was stenciled across the object in blocky, white letters.

It wasn't an alien. It was from them, the ones he'd destroyed. They must have decided to leave him a souvenir of their own.

"You know the point of no return, Gunny," he said to the soldier manning their ballistic projectiles. "They pass the mark without changing course, fire at will."

"The object is slowing," Radar said. "It looks like it is going to match velocity and come alongside us."

"Any detectable weapons?" He wasn't fool enough to be taken in by the word written on its side.

"No sir. The scan is clean."

He blew a slow breath through his nose and rubbed at his eye, where a nervous twitch had started to develop.

"Net it and bring it in. Alert the actives. Have them in full dress with weapons hot. Fields, you have the bridge. I'm heading to the bay."

"Sir, it could be a bomb," Fields said, stepping forward.

He gave her a tired smile. "So?"

He turned and left her without another word. He'd have to hurry to make it to the loading bay on time. It wouldn't take the crew long to load the thing.

...

The ball they'd netted was shaped more like an egg, an egg twice a man's height and dull gray, with a seam down its middle and a couple of holes where various thrusters or radar antennae might possibly come out. He watched it and waited for something to happen. Its metal hide creaked as it warmed from the freezing cold of space.

Circling the egg were ten of his twenty active duty space marines. The remaining half were being held in reserve on a safer part of the ship in case things turned ugly. They were very capable in any conceivable space emergency and would save those they could should the need arise.

After a few minutes within the artificial atmosphere of the loading bay, the egg beeped and opened down the seam. A pinkish-red, viscous fluid ran out to form an irregular circle upon the white metal floor. Another beep followed, and a body covered in a semi-permeable, biological sack slid from the innards to lie on the ground.

Captain Gleece came forward, as the person inside jerked to life and began to tear itself out of the loose wrapping. A boy of no more than twelve years wiggled free of the cocoon. He pulled from his face a translucent mask, gagged a few times, and lay still. He was naked, except for a pair of large, silver bands that encircled both his forearms.

The Captain patted one of the soldiers on an armored shoulder and stepped inside the protective circle. He knelt before the boy. Aside from the strange forearm bands, the kid looked like any other kid.

"Son, it's time to wake up," he said.

"What year is it?" the boy asked in a croak.

"2322."

The kid laughed. "I bet you're right," he said. "Yes, sir. I know. I will do my duty."

The Captain shook his head. "Son, are you alright?"

The kid rubbed his face with a slime-covered hand and opened his eyes. One of the soldiers stepped forward and handed the Captain a robe.

"I'm sorry," the boy said, coming to his feet. He displayed his metal forearms like they were the most prized things in the world. "I was answering my father and grandfather. Forgive me."

The Captain handed the boy the robe, and the boy covered his nakedness.

"Let's start with your name, son."

The boy sighed and looked to the floor. "What is today?"

"August 25."

"So, only a day after the final dissemination? You found me so quick."

The Captain didn't see the need to tell him they'd been heading toward the arc-habitat's debris field.

"Sorry, grandfather," the boy shook his head and looked Captain Gleece in the eye. "My name is Bill Nelson. On my left," he held up his metal forearms, "is

58

my father, Mike, and on my right is my grandfather, Richard."

The Captain frowned.

"Grandfather wants you to know, right off, that nobody is dead. He, I mean we, realize that you were just following orders. He wants me to tell you that all three million souls that were aboard the arcs are still alive and are now soaring in all directions inside their various self-replicators. They are all collecting and growing as they go. So, don't feel bad."

"Son, let's slow down a bit," the Captain said.

The boy, Bill, nodded. "Grandfather just didn't want you thinking you killed everybody. He said that would have been enough to break you down to nothing in no time."

"Grandfather?" the Captain prompted.

Bill looked to the floor again. "Yes sir." Gleece could tell the boy wasn't talking to him. Just who he really was talking to, that was the million-credit question.

"I'm a Kin Carrier," Bill said and again showed the Captain his forearm bracelets. "We found a way to live forever. These bands are why you came to kill us."

The Captain, like all those from Earth, had known the Proxima Centauri arcs had broken the law. They'd just not known the details. Whatever it'd been, it'd been awful. The Space Authority had never been so up in arms.

"You're going to have to explain that, son," he said.

Bill smiled and gazed at the metal surrounding his arms. "Some software, some hardware, quite a bit of gray matter, and different parts of the brain. All of it is connected to me. I am the engine, at least for now. My dad and grandfather still live, and will continue, forever. The tech for future transitions is in my replicator." He indicated the egg behind him.

"I was chosen to stay behind and keep to the Proxima orbit, to build and grow, and tell you the truth of things when you finally came."

The Captain held both his hands up in an effort to slow the boy down. "I saw the explosions, son. I saw the arcs destroyed." He'd ordered it. He'd stared as millions of people had died by the push of a button.

But Bill was shaking his head. "No. You didn't kill us. Your missiles simply created the spark needed to shoot us out to everywhere. To you, our leaving probably looked like ejecting debris."

There was a lot going on here. Self-replicators? Collecting and growing? He'd have to figure out the details on their way back home.

"Truly, boy? They are all alive?" he asked.

Bill nodded. "Alive and on their way to explore everything there is to explore."

The Captain looked long and hard into Bill's eyes, searching for a lie, searching for a hint that the boy may have cracked a marble and be talking in a delusion. He couldn't see a single shadow of doubt or confusion on the kid's slime-smeared face.

"Let's get you cleaned up," he said. He'd have the engineers checking out the kid's egg within the hour, and after the kid was cleaned up he'd have the doctors give him a thorough checkup, especially his psych profile.

He nodded to one of the soldiers, who ushered the boy away.

"First Lieutenant Fields," he called over his private band. "Set course for home."

"Gladly sir," she said.

He smiled and wondered what Space Authority would think. If they'd been mad before, then they'd be doubly so now. What would they say when he walked the boy up the steps of the World Capital Building and told them that there were millions of immortal men and women exploring the heavens?

60

Life would change. That was a fact.

It was true that *history* was written by the victor.

This time, though, it looked like the future would be too.

About the Author

Jason Lairamore is a writer of science fiction, fantasy, and horror who lives in Oklahoma with his beautiful wife and their three monstrously marvelous children. He is a published finalist of the 2012 SQ Mag annual contest and the winner of the 2013 Planetary Stories flash fiction contest. His work is both featured and forthcoming in over 30 publications, including "Perihelion Science Fiction," "Stupefying Stories," "Third Flatiron Anthologies," and "Postscripts to Darkness," to name a few.

*****~~~~*****

The Time It Happened

What Was Lost

by Larry C. Kay

The loud, smoky tavern called the Twisted Neck welcomed only the lost, the low, and the doomed. That described nearly everyone born in Sepenthe, the City of Sewers. The tavern thrummed with desperate business, even more so on Jagannath Day. Folks needed to forget. Forget the loved one they had lost, or drown the lump in the back of their throat that said that *they* should have been the one to be crushed beneath the great wheel.

Yvan shuffled in to the Neck with none of his usual predatory spark. He did not scout the tables for addled merchants, unable to feel their purse being snipped, or for guardsmen with a wary eye and a ready hand. He did not even check to see if anyone was scoping him. Some folks saw a boy of twelve years as a target. More fool them.

He needed a friendly face, and a hot tankard of gutrot. He chose the empty table in the corner that was rumored to be cursed. Yvan's mother had started the rumor, and it kept the table free most nights.

Big Peete, the barkeep, surprised him with real liquor, and even clamped a warm hand on his shoulder. The simple touch nearly broke Yvan's cultivated darkness. Unlike some, Big Peete didn't serve kids, but he had known Yvan since he was a runt out begging for copper and stealing shriveled apricots.

Yvan did not look up into Peete's eyes, afraid to find a softness there. He could not afford that. No one in Sepenthe could. Only the brutal survived, and the fact that he had watched his mother stand tall before the rolling juggernaut, and then fall to be crushed, was just another death among many.

Yvan sipped at the foul brew before him and brooded. He had watched penitents throw long sashes of stiff wool before the massive contraption, so that when the death wheel came they could not escape. His mother had stood without aid, and fell without a cry, exhausted from her life of despair and drudgery. *Was she tired of her oldest son too?*

"Uvng."

Yvan spun, heart ascatter at the soft whisper. It had sounded like his name, ushered up from the shadows. Yvan snorted, and wondered what Peete had put in his drink. He spat on the floor to show the city he was hard, just like he had been taught. His mother had fought for scraps, for a berth, for anything that kept them one more day in porridge and beans, far above what was expected of mothers in this twilight of the world.

Then his little brother had arrived. Yvan worried, saw his mother's belly grow, saw her diminish. He started to see the unborn as a disease, but Mama set him straight. Family was fierce. Protect your own.

His mother squirted little Mika out at dawn on a rainy day in Saturnine. And once the ankle-biter could walk, Mika was Yvan's shadow. Yvan showed him how to distract a merchant, so that he could cop a loaf. And how to string a line to lift a purse or a fancy hat. He saw pride on his mother's stern face, and he felt true warmth in his hollow belly.

Then Mika got sick. Not from a fight or a fall, just up and started coughing. Physicker just shook his head. Mika died at dawn nearly six years to the day that he had arrived in the city that fed its wretched refuse to a rolling engine of stone that ate hope and shat agony.

The jagannath had trampled his mama's flesh and bone that morning, but the light had died in her eyes long ago. It had been up to him to be the furious one. He stole, scrapped, and paid the toll, so Mama could sleep out of the rain. No more talks about escaping the city, or late night stalking where they waited for drunks, and talked of the stars.

The stars were the one thing that had not gone sour. And just like the blackness between the stars, they talked about what was missing. So much was missing from their lives, from everyone's. It was hard to describe such misery. Even words were missing.

"Yvan."

Yvan jumped out of his chair. People leered at him. He ignored them all, even the worried look that Big Peete leveled at him. Something had jabbed him. He was certain. He observed nothing unseemly, but he knew sorcery licked the cobbles for the unwary. His instincts told him that he needed to show a leg. A moving target was a hard target. His mama's first lesson.

Yvan downed his heavy, bitter drink. His head buzzed, and he felt mean and ready. He could see why folks acquired a taste. He fled into the warrens of the city as only a runt could. It became clear, however, that something followed him. It knew the holes and alleys as well as he. *Another runt, then.* Someone looking to claim his stake, thinking him distracted or grief-stricken. *Stupid.*

He ran to the abandoned mill and listened for pursuit. He filled his head with rat thoughts. He tried not to think about the time he had holed up there with Mama when the guardsmen had caught them filching from a sauced noble. As his breathing returned to normal, his mama's final fall swelled within his mind unbidden.

He had watched her death, even though she had bid him stay away. He had left before the jagannath had passed, however. What came after he could not witness. When the Scrapers came to peel the bloody residue from the streets. And when they left, the scavengers.

A scratching movement sent his heart fluttering. *Rot! His hunter was skilled.* He ran from the mill, and dodged noble decadents and masqueraders down by the canal. He jumped walls, crawled through windows, and climbed up drainpipes. Only a mongoose with wings could follow that route.

But something did. His hunter flowed from crevice to niche. He caught sight of it once. It almost seemed like a shadow itself, or a black blanket. *How did a blanket run? More importantly, how did you outrun a blanket that could run?*

Yvan panted and cursed while he considered his options. One final hidey hole: the old church. No one had ever found them there. It was Mama's best den, an abandoned well tucked in the rear churchyard. No one believed in prayer anymore, but they believed in ghosts, so they avoided the church and its graveyard.

Even as his lungs burned, he sprinted. The creature stayed with him, but Yvan hoped the ghosts would help him. He dropped into the well, and landed in putrid muck. It bothered him not at all. He sunk in it, and it cooled him, hid him.

Then he heard the sound. Not a scraping of someone trying to be quiet, or the taunts of someone who yearned for another's pain. It was *singing*. Horribly deformed singing. A corrupted lullaby. And then he knew who his hunter must be: his mother.

The jagannath had crunched her bones and squeezed her innards, and she had returned as a haint to eat his soul. Folks talked of it when the fire burned low and the herb took them.

And then she was there, soft as a breeze, terrifying and distorted, staring down at him from the well's rim. She was bone chips and organ meat and long dark hair smashed flat into a smear. A smear that moved and hungered. Yvan quivered in the mud. He would have prayed if he knew how.

"No, Mama. No."

The thick stain of ruined flesh slid down the walls of the well, humming all the while. "I came back, Yvan. I came back for you. I *know* things."

What Was Lost

Yvan didn't want to learn her selcouth knowings from beyond the grave. "Just go. Please, Mama." She was close enough to touch him. He could smell her now, rotten and acrid.

"Let me hold you, Yvan. My first child. I'll kiss away the terrors."

You're the terror. But part of him wanted to be hugged. It was too much to hold in his head. Finally he understood his mother's urge to stand before the rolling jagannath, to find an ending, to surrender. Yvan closed his eyes.

The blackened, grimy tissue that once was his mother undulated forward, and enveloped Yvan. He whimpered and sighed as she wrapped around him completely and squeezed. He shivered against her moist warmth, and inhaled the odor of death mixed with something else, something unnamable.

She clutched him, and spoke to him with her mangled lips. "Do you remember our talks beneath the stars, Yvan? We were right. There are things missing. Powerful things. Wonderful words. We did not lose the words, Yvan. They were taken from us. Listen. I will tell you."

He listened as she constricted, and when blackness came, he thought he understood.

...

When Yvan awoke, he was alone on the ground next to the well. He stank and bled, but was intact. And despite the ache in his limbs, and the tenderness inside his skull, he remembered. His mama had brought back truth from beyond the veil. That fierce protectiveness that his mother showed him, and he for Mika, it had a name.

It was called *love.*

Yvan stumbled to his feet, hungry and sore, but he felt solid and warm. He felt like shouting the lost words. *Love* and *compassion* and *courage.* He had to bring them back. But first, he had to find the ones responsible for their theft. He would teach them the words *he* had learned from surviving in Sepenthe for twelve long years.

About the Author

Larry C. Kay knows about lost words, shambling spirits, and rotgut. He shares his Florida home with a Spicy Goddess, a Cat-Pirate masquerading as his daughter, and a flambillion fire ants. Surviving in a damp, dark chamber on stale coffee grounds and the glue used on book bindings, he is, even as you read this, hard at work on his next offering. Find out more at ScribbleNinja.com.

*****~~~~~*****

Armada of Snow

by Richard Mark Ankers

Sirens split the morning, my brother and I leaping from our plastic beds to stand by the reinforced window. There seemed to be a commotion out in the courtyard. Adults ran in aimless circles, some shouting obscenities, whilst others remained silent, hugging the shadows of the high-sided walls. A few of the older ones, who I imagined had seen such things repeated many times in their lifespans, just sat on the floor and wept.

"I can't see, Torin," Sharl bemoaned.

"Hold on, titch," I replied. I picked up the stool, the only piece of furniture in our room other than our beds, and placed it beneath the window for Sharl to stand on. He leapt atop it with an energy and vigor that I'd long since lost.

"Do you think someone's trying to escape?" he asked.

"I don't know."

"Has the food truck arrived?"

"I don't know.

"Maybe one of the teachers has gone crazy again?"

"I don't know, Sharl!" I snapped, even though I tried not to. Being the eldest by almost ten years, I was expected to answer all Sharl's questions; after all, he had nobody else to ask. The what, why, and how things happened in our shallow existences always fell upon my shoulders. I made a point of answering as honestly as I could that I didn't know, or just wasn't sure. Each time I replied in the negative it lost me yet another morsel of my brother's respect.

Sharl spotted the armada first. He pointed into the clear sky with glee, his forefinger wagging like a dog's tail. In the space of a wish, he'd forgotten his contempt for me and found another target for his attentions. I followed his excited gesticulating up, and then up again, high into the staggering distance. At first, I saw nothing other than another bright morning as bereft of moisture-bearing cloud as every other. I even thought my brother crazy for a moment, to have succumbed to the madness that isolation brings. He wouldn't be the first or the last. But Sharl had not, his young eyes keener than my own.

The highly polished Sinertian ships crested the horizon in swarms of droning, nipping bugs. The sound of their motors eclipsed even the wailing, catlike tones of the air-raid sirens. I feared then. So many ships appearing from nowhere had only happened once before in my lifetime, and that hadn't been good, not good at all. The reflected me in the window glass looked even glummer than the actual me felt. But I tried my best not to show it for my brother's sake.

"There must be millions of them, Torin!" Sharl gushed.

"Don't exaggerate," I replied in a very big-brotherly way. When the things kept on coming, I realized he was right.

The more ships that materialized the greater the excitement that suffused Sharl's face, he beamed with manic glee. But like all things there is a tipping point, and when the sky was full, his joy began to diminish. It looked as though our world had regained an atmosphere, so many tiny dots were there all merging into clouds of titanium hue. The sky undulated with metallic motion, a sea of alien invasion.

We stood together at the barred window, expressionless and silent. Not a word passed between us, for there was nothing to be said. When the azure sky was no longer visible for the congealed mass of invaders, I put my arm around Sharl's shoulders. I didn't know what else to do. My little brother shook like a leaf. The vibrations from his chattering teeth travelled up my arm to stir my own into action; we rattled in unison. Where my rambunctious little brother would have normally cast my arm aside, instead, he accepted it without complaint. That was not like Sharl at all! So, I hugged him closer, unashamedly seeking to comfort him in a way I thought our father would have. I could never replace him, but Sharl needed that reassurance, even if it was a false one. There was no doubt in my own mind, not an iota of uncertainty. I was certain our world was to be conquered. Whether that included us, the rest of our lives spent in servitude, or whether the Sinertians sought to slaughter all was my sole unanswered thought. But, as per usual, I was wrong on all counts.

"Ooh, pretty!" gasped Sharl.

I wanted to tell him to stop being stupid, to grow up, but I didn't. My own mirrored, wide-eyed amazement prevented it.

We watched in awe as the crimson and emerald lasers of the Sinertian armada criss-crossed the skyline. They sought destruction in every color of the rainbow, the ones I remembered from my time as a young boy. It was beautiful, in a 'we're-all-going-to-die' kind of way. I'd never seen so many colors. But when a bolt of vivid, neon hue shot straight towards us, me cringing, poor Sharl ducking out of the way, I knew it all over for us. My only regret in those last few moments was that I still had so many things I thought I should say to my brother. How proud I was of his strength, his resilience. How I couldn't have asked for a better little brother in the entire world. I think he would have liked that, and I should have said it regardless. But the lasers did not strike the ground, or even come close. Instead, lighting the sky in bursts of exploding brilliance, the weapons erupted like fireworks against the unseen shields of our Empyrean's defenses. I'd thought their boasts of absolute security to be just that, boasts. I was wrong. When our own weapons shot into the air felling all in their path in great swaths of destruction, we both began to smile again. It was the most beautiful ballet of light and smoke one could ever imagine. I didn't think it could have been choreographed better. And judging by the look on my little brother's face, he was even more enamored than I. One by one, the Sinertian ships fell. From a steady drip to a blizzard of destruction, the aliens tumbled from heaven.

"That must be what snow looks like!" Sharl enthused. He was too young to remember the holidays in the north with our parents, when our world still had a natural climate. I still found it hard to believe that the Sinertians could and did take our atmosphere from us. They'd robbed my brother of the simple beauties in life, those that the rest were based on. In their quest for dominance of the galaxy, the Sinertians had almost destroyed it. But that was long before the dome's construction, an effort to keep both invasion and the sun's radiation at bay. It was the reason our small planet was bankrupt, or so they said. I'd always thought that dome had a lot to answer for, but now I'd never been so grateful for anything in my whole life.

It was true. the Sinertian ships did fall like snowflakes. The alien vessels toppled from the sky, glinting in the clear, unbroken light. Their destruction was an ever-increasing maelstrom of annihilation, an event rather than a natural occurrence. The things bounced off the Empyrean's invisible defenses in cascades of sparkling death. Not one of the Sinertian ships made it through the translucent dome, not one crashed upon the city's homes. And, then, in the blink of an eye there was no armada left. Almost before it seemed to have begun, it was over. The defining battle of our time had been no more than a storm passing through.

I wept my first tears in years that strangest of mornings. I didn't think my brother saw them. I hoped not. Our parents had died defending our world from the last armada, like so many others of their age. A whole generation swept away by war, their children displaced. I remembered every detail of it. Sharl was too young to recall a thing; there were times when I envied him that. The only memories he possessed were those I had gifted him. But that was no longer the case. Sharl could say he was there and survived, as I had been ashamed to for almost eight years.

The Sinertians' defeat offered a few crumbs of comfort, a few scraps of solace for the loss of our parents, but not much. Once embellished it would give Sharl and the other young ones a few months of something to talk about at the communal breakfast table. They would laugh and cheer of the day the sky snowed ships. They'd talk of a time of snowflakes, when the sky clouded over gray. The older ones, such as myself, would not. I suspected given a day or so, we'd be as bitter about it as ever we were.

I thought about all that and more as we headed back to our standardized, orphanage beds that morning that should have been of winter.

###

About the Author

Richard Mark Ankers is a former Company Director, who after winning a gold medal on the authonomy.com website resigned his post to pursue his love of writing. Richard has had poetry and prose published in *TheTopHatRaven* literary magazine and writes for his own website at richardankers.com.

*****~~~~*****

The Time It Happened

Puppy Love

by Thomas Canfield

"Sputnik!" McCarran made a face, as if trying to expel a foul taste from his mouth. "We didn't have enough problems as it was—then along comes Sputnik! This agency hasn't experienced a single moment's peace since. I field twenty calls a day asking what we mean to do about Sputnik. I'm not talking about inquiries from the press, either. These are people at the Defense Department. They are heads of other Agencies—people who matter. They all want something done. Not tomorrow. Tomorrow isn't soon enough. They want it done today. What am I supposed to tell them, Bradshaw? What reassurance can I offer?"

"We're working on a satellite of our own, Chief." Bradshaw had rarely seen McCarran so agitated. "Ironing out the remaining kinks. I can't give you a date. No decision has been reached yet about a possible launch window. But I can tell you this: we're pouring resources into the project like nobody's business. We've retained the best minds available and set them to working on a solution. They are giving it everything they've got. It's only a matter of time before we launch our own bird and remind the Soviets who the big kid on the block really is."

"Only a matter of time!" McCarran's voice was strangled. "Haven't you been listening to a word I've said? We're flat out of time! The public is in a panic. They can see the satellite at night, racing through the sky. Right over the tops of their heads! The bloody thing doesn't recognize any borders or restrictions. It can peer right into people's bedrooms, for all that we know. The citizenry have every reason to be upset." McCarran jabbed a pen at the pad of paper in front of him. "And do you know who

75

bears the brunt of their criticism? Do you know who catches the lion's share of the blame?"

"Uh. . ." Bradshaw shuffled his feet, knowing the answer that was expected of him but not wishing to stoke McCarran's sense of grievance.

"Me, that's who! I'm the number one target! The FBI is charged with ensuring the security of this country. Every opinion poll out there, every last one, suggests that we are not doing a good job. I need for that to change. I need someone to walk through that door and say to me: 'Chief, this Sputnik problem, we've got it contained. We are on top of it. We've discovered a way to move it out of the headlines and off of your desk. We only need you to give us the green light.'" McCarran fixed Bradshaw with an angry stare. "How about it, Bradshaw? You got anything along those lines? You've brought me plenty of bad news the last couple of weeks. How about a little something positive for a change?"

"It's curious you should ask that, Chief. As it happens, there is something. I wasn't going to mention it because it's only just come up. We haven't had an opportunity to properly evaluate the information. But it might be that something is about to break our way, something big."

"Well for heaven's sake, man, out with it! I am drowning here. I am clutching at straws."

"According to my sources—and these guys know the science inside and out and can be relied on—Sputnik is communicating with somebody here in America."

"Communicating?"

"By radio signal. How that works, I don't profess to know. It's all way over my head. But if Sputnik is comm. . . "

"A spy!" McCarran seized on this with relish. He shed his hangdog look and leapt to his feet, galvanized. "That's exactly what we need. It's made to order. We take down a spy, a Soviet spy posing as an American, and that will set everything right again. The papers love that sort of story. Politicians from both parties will hail us as heroes. It's a win-win for everybody. This spy—what do we know about him? Where does he reside?"

"Well, the radio signals have been traced to Council Bluffs. Iowa. We should have an exact address in a matter of days."

"Council Bluffs?" McCarran's enthusiasm was momentarily checked. "Why the hell would the Russians insert one of their people into a backwater like Council Bluffs?"

"I was wondering the same thing, Chief. That doesn't fit their usual MO."

"No." McCarran looked thoughtful. His face firmed again, and his eyes became flinty with resolve. "Set that aside for the moment. Find this son of a bitch. Bring him in. Put the screws to him. I want a full confession. This will be the biggest media circus since the Rosenbergs went down. It will raise a hell of a stink. But we, my friend, will come out smelling like a rose."

…

Bradshaw looked at the name on the mailbox again: Csizmazia. He had a hard time even breaking it down into individual syllables. The notion of actually attempting to pronounce it filled him with terror. The name wasn't Russian. It originated in some East European state, one of the Soviet block countries. But it wasn't unusual for the Russians to subcontract out a job. They made use of whatever material was at hand.

Bradshaw knocked on the door. He had brought a pair of agents along with him, big, hulking brutes eager for a dust-up. In the event that there was any trouble, they would be more than equal to the situation. But Bradshaw was hoping that Csizmazia would come with them quietly. They had the goods on him. They had traced the radio signal to his very doorstep. For Csizmazia to try to deny his guilt would serve no purpose. Whether he talked or not, he was going away for a good long while.

The door swung open. The suspect was tall and thin, with a shock of graying hair and a prominent Adam's apple. He stared at them. In particular, he stared at Bradshaw's two companions. He did not appear to like what he saw.

"Ignac Csizmazia?"

"Yes?" Csizmazia's eyes flicked back and forth between the three of them. He tugged at the cuffs of his shirt and ducked a look back over his shoulder.

"We're with the Federal Bureau of Investigation. We need to talk."

"The Federal Bureau of Investigation?" Csizmazia seemed to shrink several inches. "Does this concern my immigration status? I've been assured that my papers are in order. If there's a problem, I'm certain that we can work it out." Bradshaw could hear the fear in Csizmazia's voice. The suspect realized that his cover had been blown and that the whole world was about to come crashing down around his ears. Fear was something the FBI excelled at. It was one of the principal weapons in their arsenal.

"Do you hear that, boys?" Bradshaw turned to his colleagues. "He's certain that we can work things out." Bradshaw's tone was sneering. He pounced. "Game's up, Ignac! We're on to you. We know who you are, and we know what you've been up to. We've got more than enough evidence to bury you. Now is the time to make a full confession. The longer you wait, the harder things are going to go on you."

"I'm afraid I don't understand. You need to realize that my English is less than perfect." Csizmazia waved his hands in a conciliatory fashion. "Perhaps there's been some sort of misunderstanding?"

"Don't even think of going down that road, Ignac. Nobody's buying it. Do you imagine that we're new at this game? We've heard every excuse in the book. Yours doesn't even have the merit of being original." Csizmazia appeared more and more confused and, at the same time, more and more worried. He didn't appear certain what he was being accused of, but he could tell from the expressions the three agents wore that it was serious.

"Talk, Ignac! How long have you been working as a Soviet agent?" Csizmazia stared at Bradshaw, mouth agape. He blinked several times. His lips moved, but no words emerged. Bradshaw almost laughed aloud. Csizmazia's reaction was so overdone that there wasn't a chance of his being able to sell it.

"Don't look so surprised! We know that you're in contact with Sputnik. We know that you've been bouncing signals back and forth. How you're doing it, by what method or means, that we don't know. But we're going to find out. We're going to search this house top to bottom, every square inch of it, until we find the answers. Everything you own, everything without exception, we're going to confiscate under the Federal Espionage Act. We're taking you into custody as well. Don't bother packing and don't imagine that you're entitled to a phone call. You're not.

"This is serious business. Sputnik represents a threat to the safety and security of the United States. It has been assigned a Code One priority, the most elevated possible. Anybody aiding and assisting Sputnik, anybody facilitating its mission," Bradshaw stared hard at Csizmazia, "will be designated an enemy combatant and treated with the utmost severity."

"Sputnik?" Csizmazia looked dazed. "You're referring to the satellite of that name?"

"You know of some other Sputnik?" Bradshaw's tone was heavy with irony. "That would mean that there were two of them. One is quite enough."

"I express myself poorly. I only wanted to suggest my astonishment." Sudden excitement seized Csizmazia. "But I think I may have discovered the source of our misunderstanding. You are addressing the wrong person. If this is about the satellite, the Sputnik, then you probably want to speak to my son."

"Your son?" Bradshaw was taken aback. "You're telling me that your son is the spy?"

"No, no, no!" Csizmazia waved his hands in disavowal. "My son is only fifteen. Zoltan is a good boy, a good American. It's just that he likes. . . He has taken up electronics as a—how do you say—a hobby, no?"

"A hobby?" Bradshaw exchanged a look with the other agents. "Are you pulling my leg?"

...

McCarran gave Bradshaw a long, hard stare, a look that was, to say the least, unfriendly. "The kid is how old, again?"

"He's fifteen." Bradshaw offered a lazy shrug of his shoulders. "Very nearly sixteen. At least, that's what he claims."

"You're sure you've got this straight, Bradshaw? You don't think that maybe the old man is offering up his kid as a red herring of sorts? Send us off on a wild goose chase while he makes tracks back to Mother Russia."

"Hungary," Bradshaw said. "He's from Hungary." McCarran's expression betrayed the fact that he thought Hungary and Russia was a distinction without a difference. "And no, I don't think it's a ruse. We put the father in deep lockdown as a precaution. He's not going anywhere—unless and until we decide otherwise. Besides, I interviewed the guy myself, spent several hours questioning him. Let's just say that he's not the sharpest pencil in the pack."

"But according to you, according to all of the reports I've read, the kid is a genius. He is an outright phenom. How do you reconcile that with his old man being a slow coach?"

"Beats the hell out of me. Genetics is not my field of expertise. But I'm here to tell you, Chief, the kid is the real deal. When we broke down the door to his room and stepped inside, I couldn't believe what I was looking at. I thought I'd stepped into the command and control center at Andrews Air Force Base: bank upon bank of electrical equipment, stacked almost to the roof. It was unbelievable. Transceivers, transponders, transnationals—you name it, he had it all. The attic was filled with a bristling array of antennas, dozens of them, every one of which, according to the kid, served some sort of function. He was talking high band filters and transistors and capacitors till my head began to spin.

"The engineers who disassembled the rig and brought it back to the lab for study, even they didn't recognize what some of the equipment was or what it was designed to accomplish. One of our people, one of our top scientists, told me that the kid is twenty years ahead of the current state of design. He's not simply a part of the leading wave—he's far in advance of it. What's even more amazing is that he assembled all of these components on his own. He designed and built and tested them till they succeeded in doing what he wanted."

"Another Tesla—is that what you're telling me?"

"Who?"

"Never mind." McCarran brooded over these revelations. Far from being reassuring, they offered even further cause for concern. Was the kid sharing his knowledge with the Russians, offering them a strategic advantage that could tip the balance of military power? Was he offering the blueprints up to sale to the highest bidder? What exactly was his connection to Sputnik, and who was he working for?

"This so-called kid, he may look youthful and innocent and all. . . " McCarran paused. "What is his name anyway?" McCarran glanced at a sheet of paper on his desk. "Zoltan? Zoltan! What the hell kind of a name is that?" It was every bit as bad as Sputnik. It was worse.

"It's Hungarian. He was born in Hungary, I told you that. The family emigrated to America after the uprising in 1956. But he's adopted a regular American name that his friends call him. Alex."

Alex? Well, it was almost American, at least. "So why did he go to all this trouble? Why couldn't he just take up baseball, like a normal kid? You're convinced that he's not a spy, but I'm not so certain. Why is he communicating with the Russian satellite?"

"That's the best part of the story, Chief." Bradshaw smiled with genuine warmth. "It seems that when the family emigrated, Alex, or that is, Zoltan, left behind a girlfriend in the old village. Turns out he missed her something terrible. He was looking for a way to stay in touch, to keep the flame burning, as it were, when the Russians launched Sputnik."

McCarran stared at Bradshaw. He swayed on his feet, grabbed at the desk to keep from collapsing into a chair. "You mean to tell me. . . "

Bradshaw nodded. "Alex basically co-opted the satellite, turned it into a device he could use, heaven alone knows how, to communicate with his girlfriend halfway around the world. Those signals that have been causing us such concern, to which we attributed all manner of diabolical designs, that's what they were—messages going back and forth between Alex and his girlfriend. It was a bad case of puppy love playing out before our eyes."

McCarran very nearly smiled. The revelation lifted a world of worry from his mind, dissipated the black cloud of Armageddon under which he had been living. War—mutual annihilation—had seemed a very real possibility over these last few weeks.

"Don't that beat all. Of all of the explanations I considered, I got to tell you: that one never once crossed my mind. Maybe I'm behind the times." McCarran stroked his jaw thoughtfully. "Maybe this satellite thing, maybe that's the wave of the future. Some day there may be as many as a score of the infernal things bobbing around in orbit." Both men smiled at the absurdity of this vision. Then McCarran shook off the mood of lightness and frivolity.

"The kid is still in a hell of a lot of hot water, though. He's not off the hook by any means. He's been messing with things way beyond his province. But maybe, maybe there's a way he can make it up to us."

"What did you have in mind, Chief? I don't think that Alex will respond to threats and intimidation."

"Intimidation? Me?" McCarran professed surprise. "No, not this time. This time we take the high road. Offer the kid a deal, something he can't refuse. Wait and see: he'll come around."

McCarran watched the image of the satellite on the screen, a bright dot of light hurtling through the heavens. He was tense with expectation, leaning forward, eyes never straying from the screen. He had set a cup of coffee on a nearby table but had forgotten it, utterly absorbed. Others milled around the display alongside him, but the only sound in the room was the hum of electrical equipment and the pinging of the tracking device.

The kid, Alex, had proved to be every bit the prodigy he had been represented to be. In a titanic struggle waged over the medium of radio waves, across hundreds of miles of empty space, he had wrested control of the satellite from its Soviet designers. He had altered the craft's orbital trajectory so that it commenced a steady descent, fixed firmly in a gravitational death spiral. He had done this not out of any ideological conviction or political affiliation. What, after all, did a fifteen year old know of such things? He had acted as he had, quite simply, because he had no further need of the satellite. McCarran had arranged to have Alex's girlfriend, and her family, brought over to the United States and resettled in Council Bluffs. It was a *quid pro quo* that left everyone feeling gratified and content.

The Time It Happened

The image on the screen suddenly started to disintegrate into multiple points of light, fragmenting as the satellite began a fiery descent through the upper reaches of the atmosphere. McCarran felt a thrill of exultation, pumped his fist into the air in triumph.

"Sputnik!" He spat the hated name with an undiminished expression of loathing and detestation. "Kaputnik!"

About the Author

Canfield aspires to worry less, for which purpose he has taken up the study of children, and to laugh more, for which purpose he has taken up the study of politicians.

*****~~~~*****

Good to the Last Drop

by Wendy Nikel

The exchange took place in a dark alley.

The woman watched from behind the tinted windows of her stretch limousine, licking her lips involuntarily as the package passed from the hands of the dealer to those of her driver. Once it was in his possession, he walked backwards to the limo, in case the man might try something underhanded. The woman willed her driver to walk faster, impatience tugging at her. She'd waited long enough already, bribing and blackmailing and spending a fortune, all to get her hands on that package. Her mouth watered just thinking of it.

She didn't even make it home before prying open the package with carefully manicured nails. The instant the vacuum seal released, the car filled with the heady, earthy odor that no one had smelled in nearly six months. The woman breathed in deeply, wondering at the way that even the scent made her feel more awake, more alert, more *alive*, in a way that synthetic stuff they tried to replace it with never could. She carefully resealed the package and tucked it away in her handbag. She clutched it close, fighting the urge to bury her nose in it so that she could once again experience the delightful pleasure of the world's last bag of coffee.

…

The alarm clock shrieked in Officer Malone's ear. He groaned and rolled over, flailing at it in the dark. Beside him, his wife rolled away from the sound, letting out a tiny moan.

"Can't they get anyone else to work the early shift?" she muttered. "Ever?"

"Sorry, hon," Malone whispered. "Go back to sleep."

Groggily, he showered and dressed in his uniform. From long-engrained habit, he grabbed an insulated travel mug out of the cupboard and turned to the corner of the kitchen. Beside the microwave, his trusty coffee pot—a gift from his mother upon his wedding day—stood empty. He stared at it, trying to remember what it smelled like back then. The kitchen seemed so sterile, so un-homelike, without the pleasant scent that used to greet him each morning. He placed the mug back in the cupboard.

His eyelids were heavy on the way to work, but he kept an ice-cold bottle of water beside him for those moments when he needed to shock himself awake. He pulled up to the tan, two-story home where his partner lived and gently pressed on the horn. Officer Bountiful trudged down the steps, rubbing the top of his head as if trying to shake his brain awake. Malone knew the feeling.

"We have time to stop at the shop?" Bountiful asked as he slid into the car. "I need something, man. My wife made me some tea, but that's not cutting it today."

"Should be all right. Haven't had any calls yet this morning."

"That's surprising. It's almost five."

"I know. Looks like it might be a good day, after all." A good day being one that had only one or two early morning traffic accidents: people falling asleep at the wheel and driving off the road or rear-ending the car in front of them, because their reflexes were not what they ought to be. A good day being one that had only one or two cases of road rage, one or two employees going postal, one or two idiot parents calling 9-1-1 to try to get the cops to come over and force their grown children out of bed to go to college classes or part-time jobs.

They pulled up to the shop, which used to buzz with activity at this time of the morning, but it now looked so quiet and still that Malone wondered if it was even still open. The lights were on, though the glow coming from them seemed more like a front porch light, left on just in case, rather than a glowing beacon.

Inside, the shop was empty. The barista leaned against the counter, reading a newspaper and snapping her gum. Malone hated how gum had come back en vogue. Everyone chewed it nowadays, trying to occupy their mouths and keep themselves alert. Wrigley for the old-timers, Orbit for the young folks. Their stockholders were likely the only people who had anything to be happy about nowadays.

Malone stared at the menu. Half of its items were blacked out in permanent marker, and the other half contained new items and new prices pasted up over the old ones, prices that were much higher than anyone would have ever expected to pay for something like tea or energy drinks or caffeinated soda.

Malone rubbed his eyes and pulled out his wallet. His fingers wavered as he pulled out the bill. Maybe he ought to just stick with the water, try to make it through the morning without spending the cash he'd have normally spent on a nice dinner out with his wife. He hesitated.

Then his phone buzzed.

...

"Hey, Mel," Tito hissed from the back room.

Melissa snapped her gum and turned away from two cops who'd just darted out of the shop.

"And here I thought they'd actually buy something," she muttered.

"What does it matter?" Tito said. "You used to complain all the time about how busy it was here every morning."

"Well, if business keeps up like this, Marcy won't be able to afford to pay us. That's what it matters."

"I know, Mel," Tito said. "But hey, I've got something to show you that might cheer you up."

Melissa furrowed her brow and checked over her shoulder at the empty shop, then ducked into the back room. Tito had his hands cupped together, carefully cradling something in them too small for Melissa to see.

"What is it?" She leaned in.

He carefully opened his hands, peeling them apart like a flower bud opening. In his palm, he held a tiny, brown item that took a moment for Melissa to recognize.

"Is that what I think it is?"

Tito smiled and picked up the object between a finger and thumb. "One genuine, honest-to-goodness chocolate-covered espresso bean."

"Where did you get that, Tito?" Melissa asked, her mind racing. He certainly wouldn't be able to afford such a precious commodity, not with the wages Marcy paid them.

Tito chuckled. "Don't worry, Mel. I found it. Marcy asked me to clean out the back room and, well, apparently no one's moved the fridge in the last six months. This was just sitting there under it, covered in dust."

Melissa's eyes widened. She'd have never even thought to go scrounging around looking for random, discarded beans. By the time the public had found out about the invasive species of beetle that managed to destroy all the world's coffee crops, it had been too late to start rationing or hoarding. Within weeks, the world's supply was just. . . gone.

"You ought to tell Marcy," Melissa said. "Technically, it's her bean."

"Finders keepers."

"Well then, what are you going to do? Sell it? I'll bet you could get enough to buy a new car, or pay for a semester or two of college with a bean like that."

Tito turned it over in his hand, and then raised his eyes to meet hers. She'd never noticed how they were precisely the color of espresso. "No. We're going to eat it."

"What? Come on, Tito. Don't kid like that."

"I'm not."

Good to the Last Drop

"We can't eat it."

"Sure we can. We did it all the time before. You remember the little sample jar we used to have out on the counter, just free for the taking. Come on. Split it with me?"

Melissa bit her lip. She looked around the back room, checking to make sure no one was watching. Her taste buds tingled at the thought of the bean in Tito's hand.

"All right. Let's do it."

...

Miss Innes used to be a nice teacher.

She used to sing songs to her students and read stories and laugh. They used to draw pictures for her to hang on her desk, on the door, on the walls. They used to tell their younger siblings, "When you get to second grade, you'll be lucky to get in Miss Innes's classroom. She's the best teacher in the world."

Miss Innes knew when the problem started. It was about six months ago, the day she arrived at school to find the teacher's lounge strangely silent. It'd taken her a moment to figure out what was missing: the crisp sound of coffee dripping from the coffeemaker. She'd torn her pantyhose crawling deep into the storage cupboard, trying to find one final tub of coffee, but had come up empty-handed.

That day she refused to read aloud to her class, blaming her irritable response on the splitting headache that hammered on her brain. After lunch, she tore through her desk, finally coming up with enough change for a soda from the vending machine, only to find that they'd raised the prices overnight. Desperate, she borrowed another quarter from Mr. Pruitt, who took her request as an attempt at flirtation and hadn't left her alone since.

Spending more money on caffeinated beverages to make it through the morning didn't bode well for her small, teacher's-salary budget. Money that ought to have gone to getting a new haircut, new clothes, or new shoes now was spent on overpriced carbonated beverages that had a tendency to make her sick if she drank them on an empty stomach. She gained twenty-five pounds, and none of her clothes fit, but she didn't have the money to buy new ones.

In short, she was miserable.

She listlessly took attendance and recited the spelling words for the day. She should have spent more time on lesson planning, coming up with some fun, interactive games for the students to use while practicing their words, but even if she had, her energy was so low that the effort it'd take to teach them a new game just seemed impossibly exhausting. How was it that she used to be able to do these things with a smile and a bounce in her step? She must be getting old.

The students filed out for recess, eager to escape the dull, gray classroom, where even the brightly painted art projects were now faded and falling down, one corner at a time, as the adhesive lost its hold on the wall. Miss Innes sighed and placed her head on her desk.

She didn't even notice when the principal walked through the door.

"Miss Innes?"

She shot up. "Sorry. Sorry, Mr. Chee. What's the problem?"

"The problem," he said, "is that the bell rang ten minutes ago. Your students were all lined up outside to come back into their classroom, and you're in here napping."

"I'm sorry. . . I was. . . I was just. . . " No excuse would work. She could feel the lines on her face from where her cheek had been pressed against her sleeve and the wetness of drool on her chin. She wiped it away. "I'm sorry."

"Go home, Miss Innes." Mr. Chee frowned. "This is the third time this has happened, and I'm afraid it'll be the last. I'll call in a substitute to finish off the rest of the school year."

"What?" Miss Innes jumped up. "You can't!"

"I most certainly can. Now go home, and. . . " He shook his head, walked away.

. . .

Stu walked down the street, yanking at his waistband every few steps to keep his pants from falling to his ankles. He was antsy, itchy. It'd been hours now since his last bean. He jogged across the street to the corner where he was supposed to meet his contact. It'd been getting tougher and tougher to find someone to hook him up. Supply and demand.

He was halfway across the intersection when a junky little Ford pulled a left-hand turn, screaming on the brakes and stopping mere inches from his backside.

He cursed and kicked at the bumper. The woman inside flinched. She looked like a schoolteacher, with her hair all done up in a bun and one of those lady business suits, though even from where he stood, Stu could see that it looked too tight. Her eyes were all red, her face puffy like she'd been crying.

Their eyes met.

Then in a burst of speed and sound, something crashed into the Ford.

Stu jumped back, shielding his eyes against the debris that flew out from the Ford and the car that hit it—a slinky black limo, its hood crushed in like an accordion, now un-stretched to the size of a normal vehicle. One of the back doors opened, and out stumbled a woman in a red dress, clutching her handbag. She fell to the ground— unconscious? Or dead?

Stu eyed the gems in her earrings, her necklace, her rings. . . and then saw the corner of the bag sticking out of her purse.

"Is that—?"

The Time It Happened

Two kids, wearing aprons from the coffee shop next door, rushed out to the curb.

"What happened?" the girl asked.

"Is everyone okay?"

Sirens screamed in the distance, coming closer by the second.

The woman from the Ford stumbled over. "I'm so sorry. I called 9-1-1. Does anyone know if the other—?"

All pairs of eyes—Stu's, the teacher's, the two coffee shop kids—focused on the tiny, brown contents spilling out of the unconscious woman's handbag. Four sets of lungs inhaled. Four hearts beat faster. The sirens blared. The witnesses looked at one another.

…

Officer Malone pulled up at the scene and immediately called for an ambulance. The woman would probably make it, the medics said, when they assessed her injuries.

"Another hit and run." Malone shook his head. "We'll have to put out a bulletin, but there's not much to go on. No witnesses. Funny thing is, with the way it's crumpled, seems the limo driver was probably at fault."

"Probably just afraid that someone who owns a limo can afford a better lawyer than they could," Bountiful said. "Did you see the rocks on her?" He let out a low whistle.

"That reminds me," Malone said, "We ought to look over the debris before they sweep it up, make sure there's no other valuables that got overlooked in the inventory. Better believe a woman like that will be making sure everything is accounted for."

Together, they nudged their shoes through the debris. It was mostly chunks of metal, bits of asphalt, and fragments of shattered glass. If a diamond had broken loose from a piece of jewelry, there'd be no way he'd be able to tell it apart from the glimmering pieces of glass, but Malone at least had to try.

Then something caught his eye, something that definitely was not glass. He pinched the tiny bean between his fingers and brought it up to his nose, disbelieving what he was touching. He must have been crouched there, transfixed, for at least a minute before Bountiful called to him.

"Find something?"

Malone tore his eyes from the bean. He stood up, carefully brushing the dust from his pants.

"Nope." His hand rested on the bean buried deep in his pocket. "Didn't find a thing."

###

About the Author

When Wendy Nikel isn't traveling in time, exploring magical islands, or investigating mysterious events, she enjoys a quiet life with her husband and two sons. She has a BA in elementary education, and has lived in five states and one Canadian province. For more info on her previously published works, see her website: www.wendynikel.com.

*****~~~~*****

The Time It Happened

With Gilded Wings
by Evan Henry

"Back on Earth," Bill Pruett began, "people used to talk about *Saturn returns.* Did your dad ever tell you about those?

He hadn't, and if Tommy were to be entirely honest with his grandfather, he might admit that he didn't care too much. They had come to see the Swim, and that was what was on his mind more than anything. The two of them stood side by side near the rim of a large crater south of Scobee Mountain. The pressure suit he now wore was a little too big, too tall for his barely one-and-a-half meter height, but he could still see through the visor well enough. Tommy wasn't going anywhere. They had promised him the view of a lifetime.

A handful of kilometers behind them lay the research outpost *Ariadne,* the first and only manmade structure on the planet Vindler. It had been built over the last decade, its crew of scientists and researchers having trained for this moment since many of them were barely older than Tommy. His father's work at the station had gotten Tommy a front-row seat to the Swim; he wished that he could have been here too, and not cramped up in the Ariadne all those kilometers away.

"No," Tommy almost forgot to say.

"Well, here's how it works," his grandfather said. "When you're born--born on Earth, anyway--the planet Saturn is at a certain point in the sky. Say in Orion or in Taurus. And as you get older and grow up, Saturn moves around the sun. Slowly, but it moves."

Tommy nodded to indicate he understoood, though his eyes and the greater part of his attention remained fixed on Malac. The distant planet was small, only slightly larger than Earth's moon, about half the size of Vindler. Its dayside was visible as a thin, pale yellow crescent just above the western horizon. Malac's surface was rocky and barren, covered over with a thin layer of gases that passed for an atmosphere. It orbited Aldebaran once every eighty-five days, tidally locked to its star like a parent and child twirling round and round in an endless circle. Most importantly, though, Malac was the homeworld of the Icarus whales.

Tommy had expected a crowd, but the two of them were the only people in sight. To hear his grandfather talk, there might have been thousands here to witness the Swim, gathered together from systems throughout the Spiral Arm, watching the faint point of light in the distance every bit as eagerly. They were minutes from the whales' arrival now. As they skirted past Vindler, his father had said, they would be visible from the ground. Without an atmosphere, the planet offered the best vantage point imaginable.

"Now, every thirty years or so, Saturn comes back to that same place in the sky. So, by the time you're fully grown, Saturn's come all the way around the constellations and back to Orion."

"Or Taurus," Tommy interjected.

"Or Taurus. Whichever." Bill gave a slight chuckle at that. "That's your first Saturn return. Now, thirty years later, when your head's starting to go a little grey, Saturn comes around again. And thirty years after *that,* when you're a really old fart like me—" Tommy laughed. "— Saturn comes around again, for the third time. It's a very special thing to see, and some people don't even make it to their fourth return. If you make it all the way up to five, you're doing pretty good."

Tommy was beginning to understand. He turned toward his grandfather, breaking his staring contest with the faraway planet for the first time in what seemed like hours.

"Like the Icarus whales," he said.

"Well, the whales take a bit longer," his grandfather said, "but it's the same idea. Terrestrial time, about a hundred years go by before these big guys get started on the Swim again. That's when the planets are lined up just right, you see. Malac and Astris. I've seen it once before. I was about your age then."

Tommy returned his gaze to Malac. What must it have been like, he wondered, to have seen such a thing? And now, so many years later, to see it again? He pictured his grandfather as he might have looked back then, and he found he was picturing himself.

"Of course, no one even knew about the whales until the colony on IV came along. The first time anyone spotted them, they thought they were rock formations they were so damn still. So, imagine their surprise when these things got up and *flew* straight out of orbit. By the time I came along a hundred years later, all the original colonists were dead or senile. Or both. As far as I know, after today I'll be the only person who's ever seen it twice."

The Icarus whales weren't *really* whales, of course. Tommy knew enough about them to have done away with that silly idea. They were descended, as far as the scientists could tell, from land animals that had lived on Malac millions of years ago. As the orange giant's solar wind had slowly stripped away the planet's atmosphere, these animals had adapted. Their exoskeletons, dense deposits of heavy minerals, had evolved to protect them from the radiation and, eventually, from the ever-thinning atmosphere that had slowly come to resemble little more than the caustic cousin of vacuum.

Under these hellish conditions, one species had refused to die. More than simply surviving, the Icarus whales *wanted* to survive. In desperation, it seemed, they had forced the issue. As the radiation on the planet's surface became too much for their young to withstand, a few of the massive animals—how many no one knew—had inexplicably taken themselves off-planet to spawn.

97

They had developed biological thrusters, fueled by organic gasses accumulated at the center of the whales' bodies over their first, sedentary century of life. These allowed them to escape the gravity of Malac, and huge wings, which looked more like the solar sails used by the Jupiter ferry, drew velocity from the solar wind, steering them toward their destination.

Far away, Tommy knew, the whales had already started their journey. Nearly a month ago they had left Malac, where the heat radiating from the planet's parent star was too intense for prolonged human observation. Slowly, fighting the gravitational pull of both the planet and its sun, they had begun to accelerate toward Vindler, instinctually making their way to the planet that would slingshot them on their way to the spawning grounds near the dwarf planet Astris.

"They spawn at Astris," Tommy ventured, "and then. . . "

"And then, a few years later, when the orbits are right, the eggs fall back to Malac. There are a few million of them then. Maybe a thousand will survive, just the ones that are strong enough to survive the radiation." Bill Pruett paused. "And the impact."

Up above, Tommy could discern something approaching: a poorly defined black shape moving against the field of stars that seemed to pulsate and grow ever larger. He felt something blooming in his stomach. He thought of the terrarium back at the base; a butterfly spreading its wings. The shape expanded from what might have been a pinpoint, until it filled a substantial portion of the sky. Within seconds he was sure of it. Yes, the whales.

Their wings—fins, the scientists called them— unfurled from their sides as they approached, bright, rippling golden sheets. As they drew nearer, he could make out hundreds of the whales, perhaps a thousand or more in all, each more than a kilometer in length. They formed a giant swarm that began slowly to blot out the stars. The minutes dissolved into seconds, as the whales dove toward the horizon, finally eclipsing Aldebaran and plunging the world into darkness.

A deathly stillness fell over Vindler. Tommy Pruett heard his own breathing, alternating deep and shallow. Nothing to be heard, and almost nothing to be seen. The whales soared overhead, visible only where their wings or the shimmering surface of their bodies reflected the faint light of distant stars. Magnificently silent they flew, each of them in perfect synchronization with the others, like cells of a single organism. They flew low over Vindler, moving in straight lines, seeming for their stillness more projectiles than animals; perhaps just out of reach, Tommy thought.

No sooner had his eyes adjusted to the dim starlight than the brilliant red-white light of Aldebaran cut into the world again. The Swim had come, and, in what had seemed to Tommy like mere seconds, it was over. The bottom of the pod moved downward and out of sight, disappearing below the horizon and joining the others on the opposite side of the planet.

Tommy cleared his throat. "And the whales that spawn. Where do they go?"

"Into the sun," Bill replied matter-of-factly. "Their work is done, so they just. . . " He paused, searching for the best words. "Burn up."

"How long will it take," Tommy said, his voice breaking just a little, "for them to die?"

"A few days," Bill said. "Maybe a week at the most. They'll be pulled in by Aldebaran before too long."

"Twice," Tommy whispered, not quite to himself. "You've seen it twice."

His grandfather nodded. "And I imagine this is the last time I'll be seeing it."

They stood together, their eyes fixed again on the distant crescent. Not in anticipation this time, but in wonder.

The Time It Happened

"Come on, Tommy," Bill said, one stiff-gloved hand gently urging Tommy in the direction of the base. "Not much air left. Time to head back."

Tommy Pruett turned to follow his grandfather. They started the trek westward, their boots retracing their hour-old path back to the *Ariadne*. After a few dozen steps Tommy could no longer help himself, and he glanced over his shoulder for one last look at far-off Malac.

About the Author

Evan Henry is a writer, freelance editor, and one-man boon to the coffee industry. Though he is the editor in chief of Black Ship Books, a small UK-based publisher of comics and genre fiction, he is severely underqualified, and is currently pursuing a BA in English. After reading the rest of the stories in this collection, you can check out more of his work at: BlackShipBooks.com

*****~~~~*****

Net War I

by Elliotte Rusty Harold

December 26, 2034, the day the net goes down. The enemy launches a preemptive strike. Routers lock up. Firewalls disintegrate into random bits. Servers erase themselves. Phones transform into overpriced glossy paperweights. There is no front line. Everywhere and everyone are attacked. In seconds the country is reduced to a mid-20th century level of technology. Within a week, it's back to the 19th.

Unable to access the traffic control system, cars park themselves at the nearest safe location. Trains shunt themselves onto the nearest side track. Airport control towers mostly remain operational but are unable to talk to each other. Pilots, many of whom haven't taken manual control for years, scramble to land at any available runway. Not all of them make it. Aside from a few antique cars with collector plates, not legally allowed to operate on the smart roads, nothing moves.

Video, audio, text, email, the Web, all gone. With no long-distance communication, most people assume the outage is local and temporary. They gather in hallways, lobbies, and streets, while they wait for the sysadmins to restore service. This limits the panic, rioting, and hoarding, which is fortunate, since fire and police stations are also offline.

For safety reasons, power plants have been designed to function through a network outage. Unfortunately the same cannot be said of the electrical grid. When household meters and appliances are no longer able to order power from the grid, the grid stops delivering. Buildings with solar panels maintain some level of service. The rest go dark.

The Time It Happened

Hospitals have generator power, but most have outsourced diagnosis and surgery to doctors working remotely from cheaper countries. They find themselves suddenly short staffed. Wikimed is inaccessible, so onsite staff must rely on memory. Centralized patient medical records are no longer available. Personalized drugs cannot be compounded or prescribed. The automated pharmacy cabinets refuse to dispense opiates and other strong generics (a word that has come to mean nonpersonalized rather than nonbranded) since they cannot log the orders with the proper regulatory body.

Absent connections to payment networks, even stores that still have power are unable to process transactions. As food begins to run low, some stores give away their wares. The rest are looted. Either way, this is the last food that will be distributed for some time.

The more savvy local governments and first responders begin transmitting handwritten notes on scavenged paper, delivered in person by bicycle messengers. However there is little they can do other than tell people to remain calm and confirm that the outage extends as far as they've been able to explore.

As the outage enters its second day, gray-bearded electronics hobbyists retrieve the old-style ham radio sets that have been collecting dust in their attics and closets. They confirm what people were beginning to fear. Nowhere has connectivity. The network is down.

A few hardened military and governmental systems survive, as well as the data centers of two of the savviest and most paranoid megacorporations (though not the links interconnecting them). These become the nucleus of a race to restore the network and reboot the economy before mass starvation sets in.

The first question to be answered is why the attack was so effective. The network was supposed to be protected against these sorts of attacks. The answer is frightening. The backdoors (for there are several) that the attackers used to gain access were inserted over a period of years, maybe decades. Not just the systems, but also the compilers and other tools used to build those systems, have been compromised. In many cases, the vulnerabilities have been burned into the lowest patterns of the integrated circuits from which the network is constructed. The triggering message may have been sent on December 26, but this war has been in preparation for years, maybe decades.

Old computers and storage media that predate the earliest infections are scavenged from garages, storage lockers, and even museums. Engineers recompile and rebuild two decades of technological progress in nine days of round-the-clock hacking, patching around the compromised hardware as they go.

Slowly the network flickers back to life, a mere shadow of its former self. It isn't pretty, it isn't fast, and it isn't stable; but for the first time since the initial attack, a minimal amount of connectivity is restored to critical infrastructure.

As the economy creaks back to life, efforts shift toward defense and counterattack. Individual homes still don't have network access, but citizens gather in coffee shops, libraries, and government offices, so they can watch in real time as the hacker heroes of the new millennium fight for their freedom. The few voices who suggest that their own country may not be blameless in this conflict, that negotiation might be advisable, are derided as defeatists and enemy sympathizers, then ignored.

The enemy's firewalls repel the first assault, and the second. Visceral waves of disappointment and fear propagate through the audiences.

It dawns that it was a feint. While everyone has been focused on the front door, a semivirus slips through a less-defended gateway connecting the enemy to one of its client states and infects their power grid. As their lights begin to wink out, cheers erupt from the assembled masses.

Patriotic teenagers flock to the recruiting stations. There's a war to be fought, and they want to be part of it. Most are rated 4F after flunking the math test, unable to solve simple logic problems without their smart devices. Only the brightest and fastest are needed in today's Army. This war will be fought with ciphers and firewalls, not tanks and trenches; worms and viruses, not swords and artillery. In this war, sysadmins count for more than soldiers. The government institutes an emergency draft to bring more brains to the fight.

The war enters a new phase, a stalemate of hack and counterhack, a constant running battle between the crackers trying to bring the network down and the sysadmins trying to keep it running. From day to day, no one knows if the network will be up or down, if they'll be able to buy food and fuel or if they'll be hungry and cold.

The war drags on. Neither side is able to achieve a definitive victory. Neither side is willing to sue for peace. Suicide becomes the leading cause of death as the plain fear of not knowing what tomorrow will be like sends anxiety levels spiking. Antidepressants and smart drugs are rated Class-A critical items, entitling drug factories and pharmacies to priority one technical support and defense.

After months of frantic behind-the-scenes diplomacy, the world's third major IT power enters the conflict. It seizes control of several of the enemy's less defended cell phone towers and universities before the enemy can redeploy enough bandwidth to stop them. Only then does it become apparent that they are merely using the chaos to their advantage, occupying any resources they can take from either side at low cost. Before strategists have time to redraw their plans, the nation is caught in a three-sided war.

Net War I

The theater of battle shifts as other nations are drawn into the conflict. First the client states, then the allies, and finally any state that has network enough to be worth hacking. In the end, the gray line between neutral and enemy has been erased.

Subtler strategies grow in the chaos. Rumor and deception are the new horsemen of the apocalypse. Even when packets aren't blocked, it is impossible to distinguish truth from fiction in the torrent of spam that streams across the few routable paths. Propaganda and misinformation drown out reliable data.

Yesterday's enemy becomes today's ally becomes tomorrow's history lesson. Borders, already a somewhat anachronistic concept in cyberspace, become less relevant with each passing clock cycle, as alliances begin to coalesce around shared operating systems and memespaces instead of old tribal loyalties based on little more than accidents of birth. New lines drawn along network topologies replace old boundaries constrained by distance and geography. Cities separated by thousands of miles that share a subnet are more tightly linked than two neighboring buildings serviced by different internet service providers. Entire nation-states fall apart in the chaos. The global village shatters into ten thousand tiny microstates. Those governments that remain can no longer say with certainty who they are governing, or where they are fighting.

By now the attacks come too fast for any human to understand. In a war of everybody against everybody, the permutations of enemies and allies grow exponentially. From minute to minute, the balance of power shifts as local area nets and subnets join and leave the global network. Only fully automated defenses have a hope of keeping up, and even they are sorely taxed by the rapidly changing network graph.

Faced with a war that has grown past any hope of human understanding, the sysadmins decide to risk all on one last desperate gamble. They will physically cut the links that connect them to the rest of the world and interconnect their own networks. Then they will rebuild the network from the ground up in a new secure form that can withstand the attacks.

The preparations are ruinous, sucking up most of a war-weary team's already depleted resources, and then taking some more. It is the mother of all death march projects. Deployment is a race against time: first to cut the network before the enemy realizes what is happening, and then to restore it before the population starves.

It doesn't work.

The rebooted network comes back up on schedule, but is immediately assaulted by a new generation of logic bombs and data mines. It is hopelessly outmatched. Within seconds, it is compromised beyond all hope of recovery.

The war is over. Surrender is an empty formality. The enemy has achieved complete control of the infrastructure, economy, and government. With a single command, they can terminate rice production, reroute all fuel cells to the other side of the planet, or deploy the police to control the population.

Terms imposed by the victors are neither as lenient as hoped, nor as harsh as feared. Reparations are not demanded, and no one will be put on trial for war crimes. (At least not by the enemy. Preparations are already beginning to court martial the hackers who lost the war for neglect of duty, misbehavior in the face of the enemy, and anything else the lawyers can think of.)

Infoweapons and data bombs are prohibited. Firewalls, encryption, and anonymizing proxies are banned. Master authentication credentials for all digital systems are escrowed for audit and enforcement. Ultimate authority will now reside in the network.

Some diehards object, reiterating slogans about freedom and self-determination to a populace that has long since grown tired of them, but they are ignored. In reality, surrender requires giving up nothing more than the enemy has already achieved in battle.

The data blockade is lifted and bits begin to flow freely and reliably for the first time in years. Old friends previously isolated separated by network cuts reconnect. Families are reunited. Connections are reforged. Businesses begin to restore the trade routes severed by the war.

The rebuilding process is long and arduous. It is some months before anyone is able to map out the political landscape created by the war and start tallying up the winners and the losers, but eventually they do. The results are surprising:

Winners: No one

Losers: Everyone

Which leaves the obvious question: Who exactly has been surrendered to?

The victors in the war (if any victors there are) seem content to remain behind the scenes. The invisible overlords, the secret Illuminati, the ghosts in the machine who now control the network, and through it the world, rule with a light touch. Their presence is felt mostly in its absence.

Governments rise and fall. One administration implements policies. The next repeals them. Crimes both large and petty are committed and occasionally punished. Periods of increasing prosperity are intermixed with periods of recession. If the victors have any preferences in the conflict between freedom and authority, democracy and tyranny, progress and preservation, even a favored sports team, they give no sign.

Only when the new rules are violated do the masters make their presence felt. Efforts to route around or hide from the network are suppressed quickly, cleanly, and ruthlessly. A teenage computer whiz in the former Pakistan finds his data erased, the backups mysteriously corrupted. An MIT fraternity house that has slowly been converted into the world's biggest Faraday cage is unexpectedly condemned. A squad of veteran info warriors arrives at work one morning to find that a bureaucratic snafu has instructed the janitorial robots to dispose of all their equipment.

The network protects itself.

About the Author

Elliotte Rusty Harold is originally from New Orleans, to which he returns periodically in search of a decent bowl of gumbo. However, he currently resides in the Prospect Heights neighborhood of Brooklyn with his wife Beth and dog Thor. He is the author of numerous books about software development, most recently the JavaMail API, from O'Reilly. In addition to Third Flatiron Anthologies, his fiction has recently appeared in *Alfred Hitchcock's Mystery Magazine* and the *Sci Phi Journal*.

*****~~~~~*****

A Rock in the Air

by Neil James Hudson

On 6 August 1945, Hideyoshi Kita acted without honour or courage, but only with cowardice and self-preservation. He ran. He ran away from his family, his friends, and his work colleagues, who he knew by this time would be consumed by the blast. He ran to save his own skin, as if he could move faster than the explosion that had never happened before.

Already he guessed what had happened. He had ignored the radio warnings to take shelter from an imminent bombing raid. No one else had paid attention, and like a sheep he had taken his cues from the actions of the others. But he knew also that this could not have been an ordinary bomb. He had heard the rumours, that the Americans (and, most likely, his own country) were working on an atomic bomb. But no one seriously believed that they were anywhere near perfecting it. Even if they had, there would be a warning, a demonstration and demand for surrender before its use.

He knew that he could not outrun a bomb of any sort. And yet, his legs still moved, and he became aware that he was succeeding—that his city, which had burnt suddenly with the fire of the sun, was cooling again. He could see its sudden ruins, as though in an instant it had become an archaeological discovery.

The world had become a blur, as seemingly different realities superimposed themselves on each other. He could not tell if it was night or day, seeing only a grey half-light. There were no people, only impressions of movement. He was half aware of the city turning into an enormous campsite, of the air clearing, of some buildings being restored. Of some vast activity that he could not see.

And then he tripped, putting his hands out as he hurtled to the hard ground. But he did not hit it. Instead, he found himself on a soft mattress, surrounded by walls. He had been transported to a makeshift room, perhaps a cell or some kind of hospital bed. He rolled onto his side and saw only one other item in the room, a blackboard on which a message had been written in white chalk, in English and in Japanese.

"You have been thrown forward in time," he read. Although as he was reading, another message appeared beneath it, which made him feel nauseous.

"You are decelerating," said the second message.

He closed his eyes then, and began to sob. He had no understanding of what had happened to him, only that everything he knew was dead. The blast had taken place only a minute ago. Perhaps he was dead himself.

He opened his eyes and read a third message, only in English this time and in a different handwriting from the other two. "My name is Amelia," it said.

He closed his eyes again.

…

This time when he opened them, something had changed. There were no windows, but this was only a wooden shelter, and there were gaps in it. He could tell there was something wrong with the light outside. It was flashing, on and off in quick succession. A strobe light.

He tried to gather his wits. He was sure that his city had been hit by an atomic bomb, and that he had survived. He studied the messages again. Could an atomic blast throw you through time, in the same way that it might throw you across distance? Had he survived because he had been thrown clear of the destruction into the future?

Then, how had he appeared to those who had now taken hold of him? He had not seen anyone else, because to him, they were moving too fast to see. But to them, he would have appeared slow, immobile even. No one could have moved him. He would soon have been found as rescue teams entered the ruins looking for survivors, and people would have taken an interest.

They had tripped him deliberately, he suspected, and would have had more than enough time to give him a soft landing, and build a temporary shelter around him. The only question was how much time. How far had he been thrown? And when would he finally come to rest?

The strobe effect was day and night, he decided. They were right that he was decelerating. In the seconds after the blast he could not tell them apart, but he was beginning to slow down. He found it impossible to count the days.

There was an itch on his forehead, but otherwise he found himself uninjured. And he felt sure that the flashing outside was beginning to slow down.

And then he became aware of a presence. There was a figure at the foot of his bed. It must have been staying still for long periods, purely in the hope that he could see it. But not still enough. He could see only a blur, of approximately the same size and shape of a human being. He wondered if this was Amelia.

For now, there was nothing he could do, and nothing they could do. They could not even feed him— any food they left would rot long before he saw it. All either party could do was wait. He closed his eyes again, and immediately saw nothing but the fires of his city, whose fuel was the people he loved.

...

He opened his eyes when he became aware of a high-pitched noise, like a tape reel being played too fast. He could guess what it was. They must have been speaking as slowly as possible, perhaps in fact playing a tape as slowly as they could, but he still could not understand it as speech.

He wondered if they would have more luck with his own, and uttered a single word. "Year," he said, as quickly as possible.

It was a few seconds before he realised that a number had been added to the blackboard. "1950," he read, although as he looked, the "0" was altered to a "1". He wondered if there had been enough time for another war (for he had no doubt that the destruction of his city had ended the last one).

The figure at the foot of his bed was becoming more and more distinct. He was sure that it was a woman, probably the Amelia who had signed her name on the blackboard. She was not Japanese, and he supposed that she was American. One of the new rulers of his country.

He concentrated on the noise, presuming that she would be speaking in English. But when he finally made sense of it, he realised that it was his own language.

"Can you understand me yet?" she was saying.

"Yes," he said, as quickly as possible.

She was wearing a nurse's uniform, and had brownish hair tied back in a bun. He still couldn't make out any of her features. The itch on his forehead was becoming more irritating, although he already suspected what it was.

The number on the blackboard changed to 1952, but she made no further attempt to communicate with him for now. But as the minutes passed, he became certain that she was smiling.

...

When they finally tried to communicate again, they took little interest in himself and the horrors he had just seen, and were interested only in what might have happened to him. It was not the nurse who was talking to him but, as he had suspected, an adjusted recording.

"Where were you exactly?" they asked. "What were you doing? Were you part of any classified military experiment?"

He was unable to help them, and often just shrugged. He had no idea why he alone had been spared from death. He guessed that it was just chance, that the survivors of an explosion are always randomly selected. They had not had time to test the effects of an atomic explosion on a human being. Or rather, he was the test.

He addressed his own questions to the nurse, whom he could now see more accurately. She could not yet answer, and probably could not hear him without technical help. But she continued to hold still so he could see who cared for him. And he found that he could now count the days, for it was at the beginning of a new night when she kissed him on the forehead.

…

When finally she answered him, he knew that it would not be long before he reached normal speed, although by then it was 1953. He already knew what she was trying to say, and finally managed to make it out above the otherwise unintelligible noise.

"Amelia," she was saying.

He repeated his own name, as fast as possible. "Hideyoshi Kita," he said. No one had asked him this.

It took him some time before he realised that she had replied, "I know."

By now he was hungry, but he was not sure it was a good idea to eat until he had reached his normal speed, and he still felt too shocked from his experience to do so.

He hardly dared talk to Amelia. He considered her a supernatural being, who had whisked him from his death and now watched over him perpetually. But as he approached normal speed, he had to know what had happened.

"You won the war," he said, when communication had become easier.

"No," she replied. "We stopped it." By now he had no trouble understanding her words, although she was still running fast.

113

"Why have you stayed?" he asked. "You are still here after eight years."

"I like your country," she said. "And I like my job. And I've waited a long time to talk to you."

She must have aged, he thought, unlike himself. But it did not show much, perhaps just a few lines on her face, but he had never been able to see it clearly enough to tell.

He learnt that she was an army nurse who'd been dispatched to Hiroshima immediately after the Japanese surrender (something died inside Hideyoshi's heart at the mere mention of the phrase). She had been in the party that discovered his immobile form by accident, but had accepted when offered the opportunity to stay with him.

"How can you be kind?" he asked her, genuinely puzzled. "After such an act of barbarity, how can you show kindness to those you tried to kill?"

She had no answer.

The day that he finally reckoned he had caught up with the rest of the world, he ate ravenously. No longer was Amelia a blur to him, but a real presence whom he could touch and talk. She did not seem to be in his room for as long as he had thought—when he first noticed her, he thought she must have been there permanently—but she continued to kiss him on the forehead each night, as she had done for eight years.

...

"Do your scientists talk to you about me?" he asked her one day.

"Sometimes," she said.

He had in fact seen little of them. Most of their tests must have been in the early years, and they must have thought they had little new to discover now that he was no longer an impossibility but was instead a mere human being.

"Do they use the phrase—" He tried to remember. "Simple harmonic motion?"

114

She stiffened, and he knew that his guess was correct.

"When I throw a rock in the air," he said, "the rock moves quickly. But as it climbs, it loses speed. Finally, for a split second, an immeasurable point in time, it stops."

He looked at her, to see if she understood.

She completed his train of thought for him. "And then it falls back down," she said.

"You are getting slower."

"And you are getting faster." It was clear that she did not want to admit this.

"Neither of these is true. I am slowing down, until I reach the point where I stop, and then begin to accelerate back into the past."

"That is what they say."

"Then we must soon part company."

He could not tell if she was nodding slowly, or if it only appeared so.

…

Both of them knew when he had reached his final day.

It was becoming difficult to understand her, although he did not have the same difficulty he had had when she was too fast. He must be causing that kind of difficulty to her.

At night she gave him the usual kiss. He had long since given up trying to understand her motive for it. He had always assumed it was platonic, merely a fond gesture towards a favourite patient. This time, it felt as if she knew he would not be there in the morning.

And then, to his astonishment, with unbearable slowness, she climbed on top of him. He did not believe he could perform under such circumstances, but he found that he was as eager as she was. He had to move with terrible slowness to avoid hurting her, but he found that this was in itself an exquisite form of pleasure, and as she became more and more immobile, he found himself more and more excited. The expression that was freezing on her face was unreadable. He could not tell if it was one of pleasure or of mourning. And he was not even put off when the door opened and a semi-naked man walked backwards into the room. He had been expecting it.

The moment of climax was the still point, where the rock hangs in the air before its change of direction. For a split second his two selves merged, and time stopped. And then he rolled off the bed and left through the door, not looking back, taking the first steps on his journey back to 1945.

...

He could still survive. If he were swinging like a pendulum, he could pass straight through the year and head back into the past, decelerating and finally coming to a halt, then moving back towards the future again. In theory this could happen indefinitely, but in practice, there was always some kind of resistance or friction. Sooner or later, he would come to a stop in 1945 and, he hoped, find himself moving forward in time at the correct speed.

Provided, of course, he was not a rock that hit the ground, in the form of the blast that had sent him flying in the first place. All he had to do was ensure that he was not in Hiroshima at the time of the bomb.

Every time he passed that moment, he would be passing the deaths of his family, the destruction of his whole life. Did they know? Would his parents know as they died that he had fled? Would anyone in the future know?

And it was only then that he realised that he may have conceived a child.

As soon as he had thought this, it overran all his other thoughts, all his plans and theories. He felt now that he was deserting his own child and its mother, as surely as he had deserted his family in 1945. Amelia must have thought he had just vanished. What would her child make of him?

A Rock in the Air

There must be a way of sending it a message. Boy or girl, it was to take care of its mother, to look after her. He began to think of ways in which he could transmit such a message, but already he knew that there was only one way.

History is one long message to the future, he thought. By our own actions, we tell the future how it should act. We provide lessons, instructions, examples.

Hiroshima would be forever the centre of history. Nothing that anyone did afterwards could happen without taking it into account. All the deaths would forever be a lesson to humanity. And he must make his stand with them.

The rock is motionless in the air for a split second in time. Does it, for that, belong there?

His child would know one thing about its father. It would know that he had had an opportunity to run, to leave his friends and family—yes, even his own mother—and run. He had had the opportunity to take the coward's way out, and he had not taken it.

He began to walk to the centre of Hiroshima.

…

It was difficult to tell how fast things were moving when they were moving in reverse. Behind him was a wooden shelter in which scientists examined a human being like a chemist's experiment, and a nurse tended to her patient, unaware of the future. With such a mother, showing kindness to the defeated, and such a father, giving his life as a lesson to humanity, the child of the future had nothing to fear. There could never be another such bomb. (Of course, it was too late to ask Amelia about that.)

He began to run, aware that he was moving faster than he should be. He was no longer in simple harmonic motion. Rather, the blast was reclaiming its own. He ran back towards his people, the ones with whom he would forever be counted.

He was moving as if through a dream, and perhaps he was. Perhaps in the last split second of our death, he thought, we get one last opportunity, to choose between being the person we are, and the person we should be.

There were fires around him now, and he cried out as they grew, and burnt his flesh. And then there was only the light.

About the Author

"A Rock in the Air" is Neil James Hudson's third story for Third Flatiron, the others being "What the Meteor Meant" in *Colliding Causalities* and "Eurydice in Capricorn" in *Redshifted: Martian Stories.* He has also sold around two dozen stories to zines such as *Nemonymous, On The Premises,* and *The First Line.* His collection, *The End of the World: A User's Guide,* can be ordered from his website at www.neiljameshudson.net. He manages a charity shop in York, and lives in a remote part of the North York Moors.

*****~~~~*****

Blargnorff Industries New Employee Handbook Human Edition

by Dana Schellings

Welcome to Blargnorff Industries! What started as a humble garbage dump in quadrant 2B of the Thurbii galaxy has become the largest waste disposal company in the universe. Blargnorff has the proud distinction of being the first extraterrestrial business to open on Earth following The Great Colonization of 2089, and we are thrilled to have you as a member of our growing team!

Attendance

I. Work hours are 57 cycles per tiinokk. During that time you have 13 llargss to evacuate your personal bodily waste, inhale carcinogens, and consume fats, sugars, and proteins.

II. Punctuality is important. The gates close promptly at the start of the workday. Any worker caught outside will be eaten by the giant lava worms.

III. Employees are expected to return from breaks on time. Attendance will be monitored by the electronic tracking tag affixcd to the ear on date of hire. Tardy employees will receive a moderate to severe shock, depending on length of absence. Three tardys will result in termination of employment.

IV. Illness will result in termination of employment. Blargnorff has no use for the weak.

Dress Code

Employees are required to wear company issued uniforms at all times. This includes the following:

Bodysuit
Oxygen mask
Goggles
Helmet
Elbow length gloves
Earmuffs

Employees who do not wear the full uniform risk exposure to radiation, disease, hallucinations, brain parasites, and the screams of workers and yellow sticker waste caught in the grinders.

Holidays & Vacation Time

Employees receive 1 cycle off per 82,600 cycles. Vacation time shall be spent at Happy Memories (a division of Blargnorff Industries), where vacation memories will be downloaded directly into your brain. Choose from one of the following destinations:

Nuclear Winter Wonderland
Japanese Hornet Island
Yudwugg Brothel (Lxbrurr galaxy)
Disneyland

Blargnorff recognizes 4 holidays per calendar lftnovrr:

First Blargnorff Day
Spring Blargnorff Day
Summer Blargnorff Day
Labor Day

All holidays begin at dawn. Employees shall report to Blargnorff Square Garden for 24 hours of observance before returning to work.

Hazardous Waste

Blargnorff collects waste from all over the universe, some of which is considered hazardous:

I. Red sticker waste: plague corpses from planets suffering outbreaks of highly infectious diseases that can be passed on to humans. Use the tongs.

II. Blue sticker waste: soldier corpses from warring planets. Some corpses may have been rigged to explode by their enemies. Use the poking stick.

III. Yellow sticker waste: beings that are not quite dead, but not alive enough to be useful. May still have some fight in them. Use the bolt gun (if needed).

Payday

Payment is the first and third of every quipkzz. Employees shall receive the following:

9 tubes of meat product
6 liters of milk
57 packs of cigarettes
204 gallons of alcohol

Employees that do not consume all payment by next payday shall forfeit that payday, since Blargnorff is obviously paying them too much.

Safety Guidelines

Safety is just common sense. Employees that have common sense will be fine. Employees that do not have common sense will eventually be culled by the heavy machinery or the mutant rats. Either way, Blargnorff has no reason to waste money or further discussion on safety training.

Termination of Employment

I. Blargnorff reserves the right to terminate employment at any time.

II. Terminated employees will clean out their workspace and then be fed to the grinders.

III. Retiring employees will be given a gold watch and then be fed to the grinders.

Questions may be directed to Bzedoo in HR. Congratulations on your employment, and all hail Blargnorff!

###

About the Author

Dana Schellings is a freelance writer looking to break into internet comedy writing, mainly because she hates money and loves ramen noodles and cheap scotch. She searches the world for truth, the humor in truth, and a dress that doesn't make her look fat.

*****~~~~~*****

The Zzzombie Apocalypse

by Mark Hill

Sure, I remember the Zombie Apocalypse. And the first thing I can tell you is that "Apocalypse" is pretty damn generous. "Inconvenience" would be more accurate, but that doesn't glue eyeballs to TV specials. If that was an apocalypse, the fender-bender down the street last week was Carmageddon.

Here's what went down as I remember it, not as it's been sold to your generation. The parts about a top-secret research facility hidden downtown are more or less true, although I doubt every single scientist was as young, hot, and promiscuous as the dramas show them. But yeah, they were playing God, or at least overly demanding Mom and Dad. Something got loose, and suddenly a bunch of people had a hankering for brains. I won't bore you with all the tedious details, so let's just say a safety inspector missed a few boxes, and the next list he was ticking off was at the unemployment office.

But to claim they started terrorising the population is like claiming a mosquito you swatted was terrorising your home. People called me a hero for escaping, but do you know how I got out? I *walked.* Yeah, the undead aren't exactly champion athletes. Oh sure, at first it was terrifying to see a bunch of fetid, moaning corpses shambling towards me, but once the shock wore off, it was like having your fight-or-flight instinct kicked in by a pack of toddlers. Either option was a guaranteed victory.

I just wandered to the edge of town, where the National Guard already had a cordon up. On my way out, I saw some things that, how can I put this. . . don't exactly jive with the narrative you've been fed. I can't say I saw any overwhelmed cops going out in blazes of glory or

123

ordinary people heroically sacrificing themselves to save their loved ones, but I did see a SWAT team kill dozens of zombies without breaking a sweat, while some old dude in a suit took it upon himself to help by knocking a bunch over with his briefcase. I hate to break it to you, but "mindless, slow-moving monstrosities" versus "trained professionals with guns and bite-proof Kevlar" is not the knockdown, drag-out fight you've been taught. I saw one get curb-stomped by a child.

The whole thing was basically over by the end of the workday. Oh sure, they kept us under observation for a while, and it took some time to find the zombies that got stuck at the bottom of stairwells and whatever. But the talking heads were struggling to come up with new stories, and the soldiers considered it a respite from serving where the enemy shoots back. Honestly, the biggest hassle was cleaning up all the blood and guts.

But pop culture nerds worldwide had fantasised about the zombie apocalypse for decades, and they just couldn't accept that it had come and gone and been so terribly, terribly lame. It started slow—survivors looking for their 15 minutes of fame claimed they made dramatic, last-minute getaways instead of powerwalking into the sunset. Details were embellished to friends over beers, exaggerations were made to impress Twitter followers, and before you knew it we had collectively decided on an alternate timeline that was much more interesting than the mild inconvenience it had actually been.

But the truth doesn't put butts in movie seats or discs in game consoles, and it sure doesn't sell ridiculous, overpriced Zombie Survival Kits featuring whatever the hell "anti-Zombie spray" is, either. A multi-billion dollar industry appeared out of thin air, all because some yahoo in a lab wanted to duck out to lunch early. Look, kid, you can believe what you want. All I'm saying is that your money would probably be better spent on health insurance and beer. And stop carrying that dumb hatchet around. You look like Paul Bunyan's asshole cousin.

###

About the Author

Mark Hill is a columnist and freelance editor for *Cracked*. He also writes for many other publications, and you can find more of his work at www.mehill.org.

*****~~~~*****

The Time It Happened

Xenofabulous

by Amanda C. Davis

"The public can forget you in as few as forty days," I told my assistant Paz, mixing my own cocktail like a plebian.

"Not you," said Paz dutifully. She was wearing one of my designs from three years ago and therefore looked hideously outdated. I hated to see her tidying even the scraps of my newest creations, in the iron grip of my old ones.

"Not me," I agreed. "I worked hard to loom so large." I sipped and grimaced. Too much vermouth. "But after four hundred days, well—" I finished the drink, vermouth and all.

"You've never shone brighter," said Paz. Bless her earnestness. It was as if she meant it.

I eyeballed the loft for evidence of my supposed brightness. Twenty wireframe forms dripped with castoff fabrics. Some of them wore half-finished dresses, the shoulders sliding down like they were trying to seduce me; some, I'd only used as a place to hang my failures.

"My dresses are technically perfect," I told her. Not a boast, a fact. "And they bore me."

Paz, ever attentive, hurried to mix me another cocktail. When it took longer than expected, I swiveled to her. She was muddling mint, eyes on the clock.

"Leaving early?" I dared her.

"Oh!" Her cheeks colored. "They're landing in seven minutes. Do you think we could watch it?"

"Landing?" I said sharply. "They?"

"The Hermes probe. The exoplanetary explorer. It's been cutting through the atmosphere of Yemoja 71b for twenty hours. It's going to turn on the cameras as soon as it comes within two kilometers of the surface."

The Time It Happened

Poor Paz, with distant stars in her eyes. I waved a hand at the television. It flicked on. A few crooks of my fingers, and we had the UNASA channel. Sure enough, there was a talking head atop a tedious suit, explaining the history of the Hermes probe, its creation, the dead planets it had discovered, the hope at every new stop that this one might be the one hosting life. Like me, the Hermes had provided nothing new for years.

"The truth is," I told Paz, "I am no longer able to surprise myself. What is a marginally shorter hemline, really? A slightly sharper asymmetry, a different neckline? In the many thousands of years of mankind attiring itself, how many truly original thoughts have there—"

"Oh, my," said Paz, a hand at her mouth. Her eyes filled with tears. "Oh, we've done it."

I turned to the screen. Through inches of protective lenses and light-years of space, I saw a pink sky and forests of spongy red rushing past. The forests grew uniform, crossed with perpendicular clearings. Then: a riot of color, deliberate architecture and makeshift adaptations, formations that must be things like glass and steel and stone. And in and around them, movement.

Paz said, "We're not alone," and burst into sobs.

I advanced on the television, clutching my drink. I could not fill my eyes fast enough. Mobile beings, organic, autonomous. Clustering and parting, turning, engaging with their environment. Being alien. Being alive.

"Paz," I said. "Paz, look what they're *wearing*."

I had my hands on my fabrics before the talking heads on television regained their ability to speak. The greatest day of human history, and I was going to capture it like no one ever imagined. Everyone would want to meet them. Learn from them. Dress like them.

The public would never forget me now.

###

Xenofabulous

About the Author

Amanda C. Davis has an engineering degree and a fondness for baking, gardening, and low-budget horror films. Her work has appeared in *Crossed Genres, Orson Scott Card's InterGalactic Medicine Show*, and others. She tweets enthusiastically as @davisac1. You can find out more about her and read more of her work at http://www.amandacdavis.com.

*****~~~~*****

The Time It Happened

Credits and Acknowledgments

Illustrations

Cover image and design – Keely Rew

Ebook Only:
Lincoln's Watch – Abe Lincoln's pocket watch with secret engraved message. Smithsonian National Museum of American History.
Kin Carriers – Orion battle spaceship (commons.wikimedia.org, author: Cronus Caelestis)
What Was Lost – The last of the spirits, A Christmas Carol, illustration by John Leech, 1843. Public domain.
Good to the Last Drop – Latte art (wiki. Originally posted by user Mortefot on Flickr)
With Gilded Wings – commons.wikimedia.org. Alaskan aurora borealis photo taken by Senior Airman Joshua Strang
Net War I –Commons.wikimedia.org. Created by 3DJournal.com, website dedicated to 3D images and anaglyphs
A Rock in the Air – Keely Rew
The Zzzombie Apocalypse – Shot at World Zombie Day, London, October 2012. Author: Martin Soulstealer. Commons.wikimedia.org

Readers

Andrew Cairns, Tom Parker, Keely Rew

*****~~~~~*****

Discover other titles by Third Flatiron:

(1) Over the Brink: Tales of Environmental Disaster

(2) A High Shrill Thump: War Stories

(3) Origins: Colliding Causalities

(4) Universe Horribilis

(5) Playing with Fire

(6) Lost Worlds, Retraced

(7) Redshifted: Martian Stories

(8) Astronomical Odds

(9) Master Minds

(10) Abbreviated Epics

www.thirdflatiron.com

THIRD FLATIRON